MW00935267

HIT AND NUN

DAKOTA CASSIDY

COPYRIGHT

ISBN: 9781720113201
Imprint: Independently published

ACKNOWLEDGMENTS

Welcome to the Nun of Your Business Mysteries! I so hope you'll enjoy the second adventure for Trixie Lavender and her pal Coop, an ex-nun and a demon, respectively, just trying to make their way in the world —*together*.

Please note, I currently live in the beautiful state of Oregon, just outside of Portland. And though not a native (New Yorker here!), I've fallen in love over and over again with my new home state every day for the five years we've been here. That said, I've created a district (sort of like the Pearl District, for you natives) in a suburb of Portland that is totally fictional, called Cobbler Cove. You may recognize some of the places/streets/eateries I mention, but do keep in mind, I'm also flagrantly instituting my artistic license with the geography of gorgeous Portland to suit my own selfish needs. Some names for characters or groups/eateries/streets mentioned herein are completely fictitious.

Also, please note, the World Naked Bike Ride, which takes place every year in Portland, doesn't have an official route. According to some research I've done, that's to dissuade people lining the streets to watch (ahem), which poses public safety issues. I've taken liberties with the date of the ride and the route to suit my own purposes. So all you amazing Portlanders, please forgive my artistic license. The title worked so well with the event, I couldn't resist.

As I've mentioned in my previous cozy mysteries, there is an ongoing mystery surrounding Coop and Trixie that will play out over the course of the series (sorrysorrysorry!), but the central mystery in each story will be all wrapped up in a pretty package with a nice bow by book's end.

That out of the way, welcome to the crazy world Trixie and Coop inhabit. I hope you come to love them as much as I do!

HIT AND NUN

BY DAKOTA CASSIDY

CHAPTER 1

"*J*eeeff, Jeff-Jeff-Jeff-Jeff, slow down, little buddy," I urged his adorable puppy face, giving him a quick scratch between his spry ears. "You're talking a mile a minute. Take deep breaths."

"Ooooh, yeah!" He cooed a groan followed by a happy sigh. "That's nice, Trixie. So nice."

Yes. That's the dog talking. With a Boston accent, by the way. He sounds a lot like Peter Griffin from *Family Guy*. No. I'm not off my rocker. Jeff really is a talking dog. He sort of makes a nice pairing with our talking owl, Livingston.

Rather like mac and cheese or eggs and bacon. Except the bacon's a little tough and the eggs are a bit runny.

Jeff sat for a moment at my feet, looking up at me with his soft brown eyes, his white and tan tufted eyebrows so expressive. "Sorry, Trixie. I can't seem to control myself. My words just pour outta me like water from a fountain. I try to slow them down, but my mouth works wicked faster than my brain in this body. I always feel like I'm gonna explode."

I reached down and stroked his tan and white head. "I get it. On the inside, you're a strong, silent pit bull but on the outside, you're a yippy, excitable Yorkie who wants to lift his leg on everything, right?"

"Winner-winner-chicken-dinner!" he crowed before letting out a howl he clearly couldn't contain.

I leaned back in my white Adirondack chair and nodded with a smile. "So we'll take it slow. Let's go over this one more time, okay?"

"Alrighty-do, but I'm telling you, Trixie, it's like a block. A big block in this pea brain I ended up with."

I tried not to show my discouragement, but we'd been doing this off and on for a few weeks now, since we'd first met, and I didn't have much hope we'd ever find out the message he was supposed to bring me, courtesy of Hell. Or if there really even was a message.

Our friend Higgs, who owns the men-only Peach Street Shelter—or what we lovingly and jokingly call the GUY-MCA—found Jeff rooting around in the alleyway by the shelter, starving and homeless. So because Higgs had recently lost someone very close to him in a way that was nothing short of a painful betrayal of trust, he'd scooped Jeff up and the rest was history. He never went anywhere without him if he could avoid it.

Higgs doted on Jeff like a new father dotes on a newborn, and it was adorable, if not a little disturbing, to see a big, tough, tattooed ex-undercover cop like Higgs use baby talk to coerce Jeff into taking his heartworm pills.

I met Jeff shortly after Higgs found him a few weeks ago, at a party we'd hosted to get to know our fellow shop owners and neighbors and celebrate Higgs's official release from a murder charge, which is where Jeff first approached me with an alleged message from Hell.

A message he couldn't remember.

Now, after weeks of trying to get him to remember what that message was, I was beginning to think we'd never know, and I'd have to chalk it up to yet another unanswered question in my topsy-turvy world since being possessed by an evil spirit.

If Hell really was trying to reach out to me—and I can assure you, the evil thing inside me has reached out plenty—then it's crucial I make every effort to leave no stone unturned. I had to know I'd done everything I could to help Jeff remember if I hoped to protect myself from the forces of evil working to consume me.

I don't ever want to suffer another time in my life like I did when I was booted from the convent, a.k.a., The Great Mooning Incident of 2017.

There's even video of the incident—in case my shenanigans weren't properly cemented in history by the gossiping all the nuns did after it occurred. I've seen it; it's in the number two spot on my list of things I hope to never experience again.

I often wondered what it would be like for me, for *us*, if Knuckles or Higgs saw me possessed and found out Coop was a demon? Worse, what if a client at Inkerbelle's witnessed me in full-on possession? The very thought made me shudder.

Today, as we sat outside on this warm day in late August, on my tiny deck located right off my bedroom in the guesthouse we rented from our friend Knuckles, I tried to help Jeff jog his memory. Knuckles remains one of the best things to happen to myself and my demon friend Coop since I'd left the convent. I inhaled the scents of his luscious garden and tried to set aside all the bad things that could happen if we didn't check every box and focus on this mystery message from Hell.

My eyes zoomed in on the last of the season's beautiful blue and purple hydrangeas lining the cedar fencing, which Knuckles so lovingly tended, and I thought pleasant thoughts.

Since we'd moved into the guesthouse behind Knuckles's main house, and we'd opened Inkerbelle's Tattoos and Piercings, things had become exponentially better.

We'd found our home here in Cobbler Cove, Oregon. We had a semblance of normalcy these days. We had friends. We had a very small profit in just under a month (mostly thanks to Knuckles and his grizzled tattoo artist friend, Goose).

We were thriving both mentally and physically—all

of us, even Livingston, as much as he hated to admit it. We did normal things like have dinner at seven every night, unless the shop was open late. We watched television with Knuckles, and sometimes Higgs and Jeff—all piled together on the couch here in the guesthouse with popcorn or the snack du jour.

We went for long walks with Jeff and Higgs when the sun began to set and it was cool enough. We laughed. We talked. We joked. And then we got back up and we did it all over again the next day.

And it was bliss. We'd grown so used to merely getting through each day after I'd been booted from the convent, we'd forgotten the simple pleasures of a routine.

Now, if we could just rid me of this thing inside me—release me from its greasy black clutches—everything would be perfect.

Which brings me back to my current dilemma. How to get Jeff to remember the message from Hell?

Clapping my hands on my thighs, I clenched my fists and inhaled, exhaling with determination. "So, from the beginning, Jeff. You escaped through the same portal that Coop and Livingston escaped through, correct?"

He panted, running in a circle as he tried to catch his tail, and said, "Um-hmm." Then he stopped and looked up at me, the morning glare of sunlight making his sweet face particularly adorable. "Why the heck do I do that? Logically, I know, I'm never gonna catch my tail, but I can't stop!" he complained in his squeaky voice as he made another dizzying circle.

I scooped him up and sat him on my lap, stroking his spine to relax him. There was nothing Jeff liked more than a good massage.

Instantly, his body became less rigid as he leaned into me.

"Better?" I asked as Coop plopped down in the chair next to mine, Livingston, my favorite sassy owl, on her arm.

"Muuuch," he crooned with a rippling shudder that ran from his head to his hind legs.

"So from the beginning—"

"Aye, lass. Not again." Livingston scoffed his disapproval in his light Irish accent. "I don't think I can do it one more time without losin' my ever-lovin' mind."

Coop put a finger on Livingston's beak to quiet his complaining—something he does often, by the way. "You're being rude, Quigley Livingston. It's important we let Jeff share his journey."

Livingston flapped his gray and white feathers, letting the warm breeze catch them. "His *journey*? This isn't Oprah, for the love of leprechauns. Let's not romanticize it as though he found himself at the infamous fork in the road, Coopie. He made a mess of everyting when he escaped Hell. That's no journey, lass. That's a bloody road trip gone sideways. And now, he's somebody's pet. What's left to go on about?"

I poked Livingston in his round belly, filled with far too many Swedish Fish, using a gentle finger.

"Technically, *you're* somebody's pet, buddy. Glass houses and all," I teased, trailing my finger over his beak.

"Yes, yes, and I have the gilded cage to prove it. But I don't spend every wakin' hour tellin' ya 'bout my *journey*. Besides that, the poor lad says the same ting every blinkin' time! Nothin' changes. I don't know how much more I can stand."

I leaned over and dropped an indulgent kiss on Livingston's round head. "Then close your ears, Mouthy McMouth."

"Would that I could," he mumbled before giving his head a swivel and closing his glassy eyes—meaning, he was done with us mere mortals and we were dismissed.

Jeff moaned as I stroked his fur, holding his face up to the sun. "So, tell me again how it happened, Jeff. And be careful. We almost got caught the last time you were trying to remember and Higgs walked in on us. I had to pretend I was playing sock puppet with you—with a Boston accent to boot. Just keep in mind, Higgs is going to be here any minute to pick you up. We can't afford to have him catch you talking."

"But you're wicked good at voices, Trix," Jeff said.

I sort of am pretty good at them, if I do say so myself. "How about we err on the side of safety and just not get caught. Higgs would have a heart attack if he knew you could talk."

Higgs didn't like to leave Jeff alone in his apartment for fear he'd get lonely. So he brought him to work with him every day—which was terrific for the shelter.

The guys staying there loved him and doted on him as much as Higgs did.

But today he'd had a dentist appointment, and he asked us to watch Jeff—which we were pleased to do because we'd come to love him, too—even if he talked at warp speed.

"Hiiiggs," Jeff mumbled. "I like Higgs. He's nice to me. He gives me good dog food. The expensive kind. He gives me scraps, too. Lots of scraps. Yummy scraps. The other day he was talking about getting me certified to become a therapy dog. He talks to me all the time. I don't know how I feel about being a therapy dog, Trixie. I mean, look at what happened to me. How can I help other people when I can't help myself? And then there's my bed. It's awesome. It has a special Tempur-Pedic mattress and a heating pad—"

"Jeff…" I said, raising my voice an octave. I didn't want to chastise him, but my patience had begun to wear thinner than thin.

I offered to leave things be almost every time we went over how he'd managed to find his way to us, but Jeff is the kind of guy…er, canine, who fits the expression "like a dog with a bone" to a T. He claimed trying to remember this infernal message kept him up at night.

Jeff leaned back against my chest and looked up at me with his big brown puppy dog eyes. "Sorry. I told you, I don't know how to stop it. Every thought in my fool head just comes out of my mouth."

I took a sip of my coffee and sighed as the warm

breeze blew, ruffling Jeff's wiry fur. "I totally understand. So one more time for the cheap seats, okay?"

He let out a soft moan, scratching at his hindquar-
ters with his back leg. "Okay, so here goes. When Coop
and Livingston escaped, they escaped through a portal
to Hell none of us minions knew about until I
happened upon it one day. I mean, it was right there—
all open and a black hole. I don't even remember how I
found it."

I still don't understand how a portal is created, or
how one to Hell, of all places, ended up in our convent.
I mean, a portal to Hell via a convent? I'd always been
taught good would win over evil. Wasn't the convent
filled with nothing but good? How much gooder did it
get than nuns and priests?

I'd always felt protected at the convent from the
outside forces working toward the world's demise. But
after the tussle that went down that night, if I didn't
already have a million doubtful questions about scripture and what I'd learned in my time as a nun, I had a
whole lot more since.

One of those questions had to do with the idea that
a demon could actually walk on sacred ground. Coop
had wandered around the convent after saving me as
though she'd been baptized in Holy Water and sworn
in as the Second Coming.

In other words, she didn't have a single problem
treading on sacred ground, which meant we weren't
safe from anything if we weren't safe from the occu-
pants of Hell—in a *convent*.

Evil exists, and it doesn't stop existing merely because a bunch of women wear habits, crosses and denounce the devil on the reg.

Don't get me wrong; no one is more grateful than I am that Coop didn't burn to a crisp upon entering sacred ground. If Coop hadn't come through that portal at the exact moment I was in the midst of being possessed by this evil spirit, it would have eaten my soul. But hello—she's a demon, for pity's sake, footloose and fancy free in, I repeat, a *convent*.

I nodded for the umpteenth time at the same exact spot in the story where I always nod. "Right. The portal that led to the inside of my convent, and it doesn't matter how you found it, Jeff. That part of the story is inconsequential."

"Maybe it's not? Maybe the portal means something we don't understand, Trix."

Maybe it did. And I said as much. "Maybe it does. But we can't get bogged down with that detail right now."

"Okay," Jeff said. "So yeah, a portal. I didn't know that's what you called it. It just looked like a big black hole. Being adventurous in nature, I decided to see what was on the other side. I'm tellin' you, Trixie, the second I stepped through that thing, it closed up tighter than a clamshell. Just poof—gone."

I continued to massage his back, feeling the tension in his muscles as he retold the story. "Right. So you escaped, but you don't know if anyone followed behind you the way you followed Coop and Quigley—or whether you all even escaped through the portal at the same time, correct?"

Which scared the ever-lovin' stuffin' out of me. What if Jeff wasn't the only demon to escape Hell? What if far more malevolent forces had escaped along with him, and they'd inhabited the bodies of more road kill like Livingston had—or worse, innocent people like me?

Not everyone has a Coop to save them the way I did.

And what if Jeff didn't escape at the exact time as Coop and Livingston? His puppy age of around a year says it's feasible. That's how long it's been since I was booted out of the convent, but what if that portal is some sort of time warp, or what if Jeff's confused about when he arrived…and does it even matter?

What if I've been watching too many sci-fi-related shows on Netflix and they're all in my head, swirling around with crazy conspiracy theories that don't really exist?

"Righty-O. You are correct. After I landed in your convent, it all gets kinda blurry—sort of like a dream, you know? Bits and pieces all broken up in weird fragments is all I remember. I don't know if I had a body during that time. I don't even know how the heck I got to where I got. I do remember following Coop's scent and trying to keep track of her and Livingston. But then I don't remember anything else until I woke up next to something warm and fuzzy—something that felt like home," he said on a wistful sigh.

"That would have been your mother, Jeff. You managed to find your way to a newborn litter of puppies. Likely, one of them didn't survive and you used the opportunity to hop inside its body. You're mother must have been a stray."

"Are you saying my mother was a dog?" he asked on his infectious high-pitched giggle.

Sometimes, Jeff was like a twelve-year-old boy right before his voice changes and he begins the long, hard road to manhood. Which begged the question, what was Jeff before he was a dog and how did he end up in Hell? But alas, he couldn't remember that, either.

I laughed, too, because Jeff's laugh was nothing if not contagious. "That's exactly what I'm saying. So what happened next?"

"Well, then I couldn't see much because my eyes were still closed and I wasn't weaned yet." He paused and sighed again. "Ahhh, the good old days, when I didn't have a worry in the world—"

"But then you realized where you came from and…?" I coaxed as I looked at the time on my phone. Higgs was going to be here very soon—we had to get to the point.

"Yeah," Jeff drawled. "I don't know why, all of a sudden, I remembered everything that happened the night I got to the convent. I think it was a dream or something. Or maybe I got a whiff of something that smelled like Coop… Yes! That was it! It was the scent of her hair—smells like honeysuckle. There was a whole patch of it by the barn where we were born. We used to play by it all the time. Musta jarred my memory or somethin'… You know, like déjà vu?"

This was the part of his tale that always made me sad. Jeff had brothers and sisters. Okay, not technically, but in this life anyway—all scooped up by a rescue and taken off to find loving families to adopt them. Except Jeff. He'd managed to escape.

However, the scent of honeysuckle was a new memory. Maybe this will actually pan out. It just might take a long time.

Dropping a kiss on his head, I decided maybe it was time to let this story be for a while. "How about we stop for today, Jeff? I don't want you upset when Higgs gets here. You know how he is when he thinks something's wrong with you. You'll be at the vet with a thermometer up your watoosie lickety-split."

His head hung from his shoulders for a moment before he lifted it, his eyes looking off into the distance. "It's okay, Trixie. They were nice rescue ladies. I bet the gang got great homes—my mom, too."

I lifted my face to the warm breeze and nodded. "I'm sure they did. I'd lay bets on it, and if you knew where the barn was located, I'd find them somehow and prove it to you."

"And I'd help," Coop offered, sipping the last of her orange juice.

"But I couldn't read back then," Jeff replied. "So I have no idea where the barn was, and BTW, Oregon's a pretty big state. I don't know how far away where my soul landed was from the convent."

I nodded my head in sympathy. "There is that. So what happened next?"

"After they all got caught by the rescue, I decided to follow the scent because it was so familiar. Little by little, things started coming back to me, like my memories of everyone talkin' about Coop's escape. So I tracked her for days, lived off the land, took some handouts along the way, somehow avoided getting caught until I got to Cobbler Cove. By then I could read, and Coop's scent kept getting stronger and stronger. But the whole time I was hoofin' it across Oregon, something kept nagging at me. One night, just before I got to Portland, I was sleeping in a Christmas tree field and I had a dream, and the dream reminded me that somebody saw me escape. It was like they knew I was going to come looking for Coop. Like they knew I'd see *you*, Trixie. Like they knew you guys were all together. And that's when they told me to give you a message..."

And this was the part that sent shivers up along my spine and down over my arms. "But you don't remember who it was? You don't remember if it was a demon or maybe even the devil himself?"

I gulped nervously, trying to keep my voice calm. The very idea it might have been Satan had me up at night.

He exhaled long and slow, his shoulders slumping in defeat. "Nope."

"Maybe it really was just a dream, Jeff the Dog?" Coop asked as she pulled her dusky red hair up into a bun, her slender fingers twisting the elastic band around the thick strands. "Maybe you didn't really get a message at all?"

"Ya know…" he started, then stopped and gave his head a shake, making his ears flap. "Nope. I'm pretty sure that happened, but every time I get to the part where the person is about to tell me what the message is, I wake up. That dream is what helped me remember what happened just before I stepped through that portal, Coop. I know I'm right. That part really did happen. Swear."

Coop reached over and ran a hand over his head, giving him an odd look. This week, she was working on her sympathetic expressions. They still came off a little pained, but she was getting there—and it was better than her grimace of a smile by a long shot. That still looked like she'd eaten something bad.

"You're a good boy, Jeff the Dog. A very good boy. Would you like a cookie?" she asked, driving a hand into the pocket of her black leather pants and pulling out a bone-shaped treat.

"I'd rather have a steak."

"But they're the soft ones," she enticed, waving it under his nose.

He scoffed. "Made out of oats and dandelion shoots."

"Higgs just doesn't want you to get fat. You heard what the vet said," I reminded him with a smile, chucking him under the chin.

"Yeah, yeah," he groused. "More exercise, fewer hot

15

dogs. Does Higgs have to listen to everything that crazy old coot tells him? I might look like a dog, but I still have the taste buds of a man, and this man wants a steak. A big, juicy, rare steak."

Coop tapped his paw. "You be grateful, Jeff. Higgs just wants you to live a long, healthy, enriched life. He takes very good care of you. Everyone should be so lucky to have a Higgs."

Coop had fallen in deep like not only with Knuckles but with Higgs. As she watched the way he cared for the men who inhabited his facility, as she watched his dedication to helping feed the homeless, saw him help them with rehabilitation and finding jobs and purpose within the community, her admiration grew.

And I had to admit, mine had, too. We'd come a long way since I'd accused him of murdering our last landlord, Fergus McDuff. We'd definitely become friends in the short time since we'd arrived in Cobbler Cove, and that was really nice.

"Coop's right, Jeff. Higgs only wants what's best for you, bud," I reminded.

"What does Higgs want?" His voice, now not only welcome but familiar, sounded through Knuckles's small backyard.

"Higgs wants to feed Jeff a big steak," Jeff called out, making me pinch him lightly.

"Knock it off, troublemaker!" I whisper-yelled.

As Higgs came around the corner of the main house, he smiled at us. Tall and powerful, his strides ate up the small area from the main house to our little haven.

His dark hair, trimmed just above his ears, gleamed in the sun. One bulky, tattooed arm swung at his side while the other hand held a cup carrier from our favorite coffee place, Betty's.

"Morning, ladies. I brought coffee as a thank you for watching my little buddy."

I gave Jeff a small nudge so he'd remember to greet Higgs the way most dogs would greet the owners they were supposed to love. As a dog, he had some things down pat. Others? Not so much. He was a work in progress much like all of us.

Jeff grunted before hopping off my lap and standing on his hind legs, jumping excitedly on Higg, who reached down to give his head an affectionate scruff. "How are you, buddy? Didja miss me?" he asked in that weird voice meant specifically for Jeff.

"You brought the nectar of the gods for us?" I asked, batting my eyelashes at him as I twirled my hair in my comical bid to be flirtatious.

Of course, I was jokingly being flirty. We were just friends, but it was fun to try out some of the feminine behaviors I'd never been able to utilize when I was a nun. I looked ridiculous, of course, but whatever.

He grinned, driving a hand into his pocket as Jeff settled by his feet, winding his tail around Higgs's leg. "It is. I got your favorite, Sister Trixie, and some ice-cold OJ for Coop."

Coop peered up at him, her green eyes glittering as

she took the orange juice. "You're very nice, Higgs. I like you so-so much."

Coop was also working on expressing her emotions to everyone around her—we were still working on what was appropriate and what was a little too Terminator, but we were getting there. Though, I had to give it to my demon. She lived every day like she wouldn't see another, and she spoke her heart in the same vein.

Higgs gave her a pat on the back with his infamous smile, the vivid tattoo on his forearm of skulls with red bandannas and a colorful eagle taking flight standing out under the morning sun. "I like you, too, Coop. So, you girls ready for World Naked Bike Ride day?"

Every year, Portland hosts a World Naked Bike Ride, where bikers from all over participate. The route is typically undisclosed until the last minute to avoid gawkers, but we'd heard a rumor it might pass right by our shop, and we wanted to be ready on the off chance someone might want a tattoo to commemorate their experience.

Plus, Knuckles had some celebrity clients flying in from LA today to participate in the ride, and we wanted to put our best foot forward in his honor. I'd been up sketching late into the night so I'd have something new to show his friends.

Coop frowned. "Tell me again why everyone rides bikes with no clothes on, Higgs. Seems to me, your tender bits would get all scraped up."

Higgs threw his head back and laughed, the exposed length of his bronzed throat strong and supple. "I imagine one's tender bits take a beating. However, the ride is sort of a protest against the use of oil and what it does to the planet—and it's also about body positivity. About being comfortable in your skin. Both good causes, right?"

She frowned harder, the lines in her forehead going deep in her tanned skin. "I don't understand being uncomfortable in your skin. I like my skin." To emphasize her statement, she tugged at the flawless flesh of her face.

I patted her on the arm—her long, slender, perfect arm. "That's because your skin is perfect, Coop. Not everyone is as lucky or as comfortable, and we have to try and be sensitive about their feelings," I reminded her, sitting up straighter when I thought about the flabby flesh of my thighs encased in my overalls.

Coop cocked her head at me, the length of her neck swan-like. "Everyone should just be happy to *have* skin. I know people in Hell who don't have any—"

I interrupted her by coughing really hard, pretending I had something caught in my throat—a clear signal to Coop she was about to spill the beans.

"You know people in Hell, Coop?" Higgs asked, though his face clearly said he was teasing her.

Immediately she sat up straight, recognizing her goof. "Doesn't everyone?"

Higgs laughed his husky laugh, and I followed suit.

We couldn't afford to be found out. Not when our relationships here in Cobbler Cove were all so new. I mean seriously, how do you tell your new friends you're possessed by an evil spirit, your owl had rein-carnated himself in the body of some random road kill, your best friend's an escapee from Hell and a demon, and the dog your new friend loves so much can talk?

You don't.

That's how.

CHAPTER 2

*W*e'd arrived at Inkerbelle's late in the afternoon to find Knuckles in a tizzy, with Goose trailing behind him. Knuckles had some very important clients flying in from LA today, and he wanted to impress them with his new place of employment—which meant we had to have everything perfect.

In light of the fact that his happiness was so important to us, especially as of late, we indulged him. Knuckles had been missing his wife something fierce these days, and his melancholy showed up in the times he thought none of us were looking.

Grief comes in batches sometimes, and I think flying back and forth to LA, and spending so much time with his daughter and her family, had him missing the love of his life. His wife Candice, who he'd lost to cancer.

But today he was pumped and rarin' to go and that made my heart smile.

Though, I have to say, seeing our usually calm knight in shining leather running around straightening magazines and fluffing pillows was equal parts adorable and a little disconcerting.

In another tragedy of epic proportions (if you listen to Knuckles, anyway), we were out of coffee.

The horror.

It's a special blend Knuckles had specifically asked us to have on hand for one particular client, and I'd completely forgotten it when I ran errands yesterday.

So now that we were headed toward early evening, and we'd watched several batches of bikers ride by while we peeked through our fingers, I was rather in a rush to have everything in place as I headed for the glass door of the shop, now etched with the Inkerbelle's insignia. Just looking at it each day as I unlocked the door and pushed my way inside, smelled the scent of ink and freshly painted walls, brought such pride to my heart.

It had taken a village to pull it off, but we'd done it with the help of Higgs and Knuckles and our shop owner friends along Peach Street. And it was perfect. The walls were bold and bright, the floors were shiny and clean, and the tattoo stations had every necessity a tattoo artist needs. We still had some work to handle in the loft above, but that would happen in time.

As I made my way to the door, my purse strap thrown over my neck, Coop stopped me at the threshold.

"Sister Trixie Lavender, close your eyes!"

I tried to peer around Coop's unicorn-tattooed shoulder revealed by her off-the-shoulder Inkerbelle's T-shirt, to see what she meant, but she stepped in front of me.

"Coop? Why are you keeping me from leaving the shop? We need more coffee for our clients, and we need it soon or Knuckles is going to go airborne from the steam coming out of his ears. Now, what's the problem?"

"I said *close your eyes*, Sister Trixie Lavender. I must speak with you before you leave," she growled in a low hum of words, forcing me to take a step back.

And that's the one caveat to her insane beauty. She'll eat your face off in half a second flat if she feels as though you're threatening her or anyone she cares about.

I think I've mentioned before, but it bears repeating: to say she's a lethal weapon is to say Hiroshima was a small puff of smoke in the distant sky. However, she'd never hurt me, and she certainly didn't frighten me.

"What's wrong, Coop?" I paused a moment before suspicion set in, and I narrowed my eyes. "Wait. You didn't get into another argument with Livingston again, did you? You have to stop teasing him about being road kill, Coop DeVille. It drives him bananas."

Livingston was quite the attraction around Peach Street these days. Gone were the days when we had to leave him home or hide him away. Everyone wanted to meet the cranky rescue owl. Yes. We'd made up a story about him and how he'd come to be ours, but sometimes, as I explained to Coop, you have no choice if you want to blend in.

He spent his days perched on a gorgeous shellacked branch Knuckles bought and mounted to the wall, where his captive audience could adore him and shower him with endless compliments.

"I did not have an argument with Livingston," Coop promised, her gaze returning to its normal expressionless dead stare. "I promised you I would try not to allow him to bait me into any more debates about what's messier—runaway soul catching or the lava pit on the fourth level. Unless he eats my potato chips—the sour cream ones, not the barbecue. Then I promise you, we will argue, Sister Trixie Lavender."

I smiled and gave her lean, razor-sharp cheekbone an affectionate pinch. "I'm so proud of you for restraining yourself. Now, why are you still addressing me by my former title?"

She frowned. As you know, Coop's not capable of many facial expressions, but the frown she had down pat. "You said you aren't a nun anymore, so I don't need to call you Sister Trixie."

Now I was concerned. In times of stress, which were rare for my Coop, she sometimes reverted back to old habits. "That's right. So what gives?"

Coop sighed, the curtain of her glorious hair swishing about her face. "Sometimes I forget. I can't seem to remember to only call you just Trixie. When I learn a name, I learn the whole thing because for instance, in Hell, there are a lot of Mikes. I mean, *A. Lot*. You absolutely do not want to interrogate and torture the wrong Mike, if you understand my meaning."

I gulped a hard swallow. I was afraid to ask what that meant and how Coop was connected to it, because for the most part, she's a lamb until provoked. She doesn't talk much about her life in Hell and I don't pressure her to tell me.

That Hell truly exists is enough for me to wrap my brain around without getting into the finer details—for now, that is. I'm still of the mind we'll eventually have a nice long talk and hash out her life before we became friends.

Coop's odd nature—her habit of addressing people by their full names, her mispronunciation of words—often wrought equally odd looks from folks. But that usually faded the moment they realized how stunning she is, and then they forgot all about the fact that she's addressed them as though she were a robot trained to speak via some software program.

"Hmm. Mike is a very common name. Were there a lot of Bobs, too?"

She rolled her eyes at me in disgust—or at least I think it was disgust. "So many it'd make your head spin. I don't mean that literally. Because I *can* make your head spin—*literally*. I mean that figuratively, of course."

"Of course," I replied as she inched in front of me, continuing to block the shop's door. "So is the name thing causing you stress, Coop? Because it's not that big a deal."

Now she leaned back on her booted heels and grimaced. "Not stress exactly. I don't know how to identify stress with any accuracy. I only know I'm trying so-so hard to fit in, Trixie Lave— Er, Trixie. I practice blending in every day—with our clients, with our new friends. I still read ten pages of the dictionary every day, too. I don't think I'll ever get to the letter Z. But I do it so I can learn and be more efficient when I blend with," she leaned in and whispered, "the *humans*."

Gosh, maybe I'd been pushing too hard? Or maybe Coop was becoming more human that I thought.

I squeezed her arm in sympathy. "Yes. Blending is important. But you're doing great, Coop. Girls Scout's honor," I offered on a wink.

And for a demon with zero people skills, she truly was doing a pretty good job of acclimating. We had some tweaking to do, but we worked each day to be better people, myself included, but I didn't want her stressed out.

Coop frowned again, the deep lines in her forehead creasing. "I don't know if I'm doing a very good job. Sometimes I struggle with words. Especially slang words. For example, mansplaining. What the devil is that again?"

I scratched my head, latching on to a piece of my very ordinary, shoulder-length brown hair, noting the ends needed a trim—among the many things on my person needing tending.

"How about we save that for another time? I have to run to the market down the street and grab some coffee. Today's a big day for Knuckles—and us, too—and we want to be ready for potential customers, right? Hot coffee is a must after riding your bike naked."

"Yes. The World Naked Bike Ride is very big indeed. But even after Higgs explained it, I still don't understand why you have to do it in your born day suit."

"Birthday suit," I corrected, growing more worried about her mental state. "And I don't understand either, Coop. But if we're lucky, there'll be people who want to commemorate their ride with a tattoo. That means we have to be ready."

"Yes. Knuckles's very important friends are coming in from Los Angeles to see him after the ride and they might want me to tattoo them."

Now my demon's lithe body went slightly rigid, her spine straight, her facial expression tight. Meaning, she was a little bit excited at the prospect of inking a celebrity tattoo.

Like I said, Knuckles is our knight in shining leather. We'd both taken to him straight away, and each day we spent with him, he grew more dear to us. His Santa Claus-like laugh, his round belly, his warm smile, were all things both Coop and I looked forward to seeing every day.

Squeezing Coop's arm again, I smiled at her and vaguely made a mental note to set the satellite radio to a seventies station. "Is that was this is all about? You're excited about tattooing someone famous and it's stressing you out a little?"

Her startlingly green eyes narrowed when she scoffed at me, sucking in her cheeks. "I don't care if they're famous, Trixie. I just want to tattoo as many people as I can so they don't ever have to suffer like you do. We cannot let Satan win. I will not let him win."

Ah. Now we were getting down to the nitty-gritty. Coop's determination to keep everyone's soul intact so it can't be bartered or stolen by Satan.

As Satan's head tattoo artist, responsible for branding every soul to enter Hell, she knew her stuff. And according to her, many of the souls she tattooed were tricked into a shoddy bargain with good old Beelzebub.

She works tirelessly to prevent the same from happening to future souls with some special ink she's concocted, courtesy of Hell. No one will ever know what she's doing to save the world one tattoo at a time, but it's proof that what I say is true. Her heart is pure—even if her lust for blood is savage.

"You know, Coop, if you listen to some of the rumors people tell about Hollywood, some of these celebrities have already sold their souls for fame and fortune. Maybe you can't save them?"

"That's horse pucky. Only Beyonce did that."

I blinked. "Seriously?"

She poked my arm, driving a finger into the doughy flesh of my pec. "No. That was a joke. I'm trying to make people laugh because I still can't smile. Everyone will always think I'm angry if I can't smile, Trixie. Knuckles's friends will think I'm angry. I don't want him to be displeased. Especially since lately he's been so sad about Candice. He misses his partner. I like him so-so much. I don't like seeing him sad when he thinks we're not looking. Also, it's no good if we hope to bring in new clientele. But no matter how hard I try, I can't do it without help." She pulled up the corner of her mouth and held it there. "See?"

I laughed and pulled her hand away from her mouth. Practicing smiling was something else she did every day. Do you have any idea what it's like for mediocre me to share a bathroom mirror with ethereal Coop?

"No one will think you're angry if you keep the tone of your voice light. We've worked on inflection. You'll be fine. Now stop pulling on your pretty face or it'll get stuck like that."

"It will not. That's a lie. What did you say about lying?" she asked indignantly, as though the grasshopper was about to teach her sensei a lesson.

"Oh, Coop," I teased, patting her cheek. "It's not a lie-lie. It's not one that affects others. It's just an expression, if you will. My mom used to say that to me all the time."

She shook a lean finger at me. "I don't understand human expressions and metaphors and analogies. Well… Maybe I understand analogies. But that's not the point. Lying is very wrong, Trixie. You know it is. No matter the circumstances."

I suppose, in Coop's black and white world, any tiny, inconsequential fabrication was a lie.

Thus, I conceded. "Fine. You win that round. That's a lie. Your face won't stay like that, but I wish you'd just give yourself some time and let it happen organically. I bet it will if you wait it out."

"Are you appeasing me?"

"Is that the word you learned from the dictionary today?"

"It is. There are a lot of words that begin with the letter A."

Thumping her on the back, I nodded my approval. "Nice job, pal. And no. I'm not appeasing you. I'm letting you win this argument. Do so gracefully, would ya?" I said with a nudge and a smile.

Suddenly, her eyes grew somber again. "You're always so worried about me, I forgot to ask, how do you feel today, Trixie?"

"*Feel*? What do you mean?"

She scrunched up her pert nose and gave my shoulder a light shove. "You *know* what I mean."

I guess I sort of did. It was a little stressful to wander around with this ticking time bomb inside of me and worrying someday I'd have an episode and have to tell Higgs or Knuckles the ugly truth. How many ex-nuns do you know who are full-on possessed by an evil spirit that entered their body when a portal from Hell opened up right in the middle of their convent?

I'm betting the number is zero, and I'm also betting most people would like to keep it that way.

We still haven't pinpointed what triggers my possession, and it hasn't happened again since an incident under the Hawthorne Bridge, but that meant nothing. Whatever lurked inside me had no schedule and no warning when it made an appearance. But so far, we have a lot of x's on the calendar to mark the days since Trixie's last possession.

"Trixie," Coop pressed. "How do you feel?"

I leaned in to her to whisper, "Well, I don't want to smash any brick walls or leap tall buildings."

"Are you making a funny?"

"I am," I said with a grin, twisting my sore neck on my shoulders to ease the aches after spending long nights sketching potential designs for tattoos.

Because I had to joke, or I'd curl up in a corner and give up. I refuse to give up. I want to know what this thing wants from me, and what that relic allegedly belonging to the archangel Gabriel has to do with it. I know this possession has something to do with that statue.

Coop threw her head back, revealing her slender throat, opened her full mouth wide, and fake-laughed. She was clearly hellbent on nailing down laughter today.

I eyeballed her until she was finished, crossing my arms over my chest. "Can I be honest?"

"I would expect nothing less of you."

"Are you still watching *Dynasty?*"

Coop sighed, tucking her hair behind her ears. "I am. Joan Collins does that laugh all the time when she's going to do something hideously deceptive to poor Crystal Carrington—her greatest foe. She's amazing. But I've watched it over and over and I just can't seem to get her laugh right."

I sighed. I mean really, where do I begin to explain the nuances of a joke and subjective humor? Today was not the day.

"Stop watching *Dynasty* and just be yourself. Be the Coop everyone loves, even if she doesn't laugh very often. Though, if you feel like laughter is necessary, maybe a little less devilish glee would help."

"You still haven't answered my question, Trixie. How do you feel? Do you feel stressed or displeased?"

"I don't feel possessed, if that's what you mean."

And that's what she meant. But if she were already stressed about learning to smile, and Knuckles's friends coming to pay him a visit, and life in general here on Earth, I wouldn't have her worrying about me.

Her finely arched eyebrow rose. "Do you mean it?"

I wiggled my pinky finger at her. "Pinky swear."

Coop stared at me, her gaze blank. "I don't understand."

I grabbed her stiff, unyielding pinky and wrapped it around mine. "This is a pinky swear."

"Is it like an oath or a vow? We have to be careful about those things, Trixie."

Laughing, I shook my head. "It's not like that at all. Children do it sometimes when they make a promise they truly mean. It's like sealing the deal."

"But you're not a child. You're much too old to be a child. You have a wrinkle by your right eye. Children don't have wrinkles."

I sighed. That was also true. Likely, the wrinkle had come from demonic possession and having to explain pinky swears.

"How about I explain pinky swears and mansplaining later? For now, I have to go get that coffee before Knuckles flips his lid."

"Trixie?" Knuckles's voice boomed from behind me, his feet shuffling toward us from the back of the shop. As I watched him approach over my shoulder, I took one of many moments I'd had recently to appreciate how perfect the shop had turned out.

The royal blue couch with throw pillows, the funky colorful walls, the wood-framed pictures of tattoos Knuckles and Goose had done, the tattoo stations, neatly laid out with chairs and equipment, all made our new space perfect.

Turning fully to face him, I smiled as he approached, his face red, his eyes questioning. "What's up? And where's Goose?"

Goose, a.k.a. Barney Twilly the Third, is the newest addition to the Inkerbelle's crew. He was tall and lanky, grizzled and mostly somber in demeanor. He'd recently turned his life around and become sober after a six-month-long stint in rehab.

More importantly, he was a close friend of Knuckles, who'd vouched for not only his superior talent, made better by his sobriety, but his hard work to become clean and stay clean after years of hard drinking. And we'd decided, if he was a friend of Knuckles, he was a friend of ours.

Knuckles hitched a beefy thumb over his shoulder, his vivid sleeve tattoo flashing in the early evening sun pouring in from the door behind Coop. "He's back there making sure there are fresh paper hand towels in the bathroom."

Goose was fastidious about the upkeep of not only his station, but anywhere he could keep his hands busy. He claimed organization and order helped keep him clean, and who am I to tell a man he can't scrub a toilet if it soothes him?

"Do you need me to grab the coffee? You've been lollygaggin' over here for ages. Fester just texted me and said there's another batch of bikers heading this way."

Fester Little owns the vacuum repair shop, Suck It Up, right up the way from us, and he'd been over at Betty's place, sipping coffee and watching the ride. The participants appeared to be slowing down a bit, mostly riding by in small groups with longer breaks in between.

According to Delores, once the ride was over, that was when the fun began and it became one big party. We'd decided to stay open late just for the occasion, hoping to cash in on the fun.

To look at Knuckles, I'd almost think he was as nervous as we were about his clients coming in from LA. His client list wasn't just vast, it was treasured. He treated these people as well as he treated family, and in his words, he couldn't wait to show off Coop's insane talent to his friends.

That he wanted everything to be perfect for their arrival made sense, and as payment for his never-ending generosity, we wanted it to be perfect, too.

Perfect meant getting that freshly ground specialty coffee from Delores at Betty's. She had the perfect blend for this particular group of clients Knuckles planned to entertain.

"Nope, I got this. Why don't you guys watch the bikers, and I'll be back in a jiff."

Knuckles's broad, cheerful face went crimson. "Because they're naked."

I giggled. Oh, indeed they were. We'd seen the lot of them at the beginning of the route just a couple of hours ago as they'd prepared to jettison off, their dangly bits swinging in the wind. There were lots and lots of butt-ox, as Coop would say.

I patted his arm, my hand covering his flushed skin momentarily. "Are you a little shy about all this nudity, Knuckles?"

He cleared his throat and rocked back on the heels of his worn cowboy boots, driving his hands into the pockets of his leather vest and blustering a reply. "I'm not. But you should be. You were a nun, young lady."

Coop patted his back with a thump in her unique way of showing sympathy. "It's just skin, Knuckles."

"Yeah," I teased, grinning at him. *"It's just skin."* Though, I have to admit, their nudity unnerved me a little, too. I don't know that I'll ever be that free with my body. But I'll heartily applaud their mission—with my clothes on, that is.

He scoffed, ignoring our jokes. "Are you going to get that coffee or not, Trixie girl?"

"I am. Anything else, sire? A suckling pig, mayhap?"

He chuckled, his white teeth flashing when his lips moved into a warm smile. "Knock it off, goofball. I just want things to be nice for my clients, that's all."

I tweaked his fleshy cheek and sighed. "I know you do. That's why we love you so much. And now, I'm off. See you in a bit."

As I swung back around toward the door, straightening the strap on my purse, Coop was there in front of me again, once more blocking me from leaving.

"Coop! What gives? I have things to do. You heard Knuckles. His guests will be arriving soon. We don't want un-caffeinated guests, do we? Remember we talked about good customer service?"

"Yes. You said the customer is almost always right, with few exceptions. But that's not what we're talking about now. So please, I asked you to close your eyes, Trixie," she repeated.

"I know, but *why?*"

She crossed her arms over her chest and widened

her stance. "Because you can't see what's outside the door."

What the frickety-frack? I looked up at her in utter confusion. "Okay, Coop. What the what, friend? Why can't I see what's outside the door?" I attempted to scoot around her, ducking and dodging, but Coop was too quick for a mere mortal like me.

"Trixie Lavender, I said don't go outside!" she almost shouted, making me jump.

I hopped, trying to get a glimpse of what was beyond the glass door, but I couldn't see anything other than the backsides of a small group of bikers riding by around her supermodel stature.

"Coop!" I warned, becoming frustrated. "I have to go. Now, please let me pass!"

"I will not."

"Fine," I said, making my body go a little loose as though I were going to back off—until I saw her face relax.

Then I faked her out by scooting around her and pushed open the door with a grunt.

And then I fell.

Hard.

Over the prone, unmoving body.

The prone, unmoving, *naked* body.

A male naked body, if you're wondering.

Coop stuck her head out the door and scowled, using a finger to shake admonishment at me. "See?" she said in a distinct neener-neener-neener tone. "I told you not to go outside, didn't I, Trixie Lavender?"

CHAPTER 3

I crashed to the ground with a hard grunt, smacking my right hip on the hard sidewalk as I did. Instantly, I scrambled to roll over, and instead found myself face to face with the man who lay crumpled on the ground, his blue eyes sightless and glassy, his white-blond hair glued to his head from perspiration.

Panicked, I used my palms in an attempt to lift myself upward, but the strap of my purse had wrapped around me, tangling up and twisting around my waist.

As I tried to untangle myself and avoid the man, the very *naked* man, on the ground at the same time, the palm of my hand leaned on something sharp like glass, cutting my flesh with a scratchy jab.

"Ow!" I cried out at the stinging pain, instantly pressing my palm to my thigh to thwart the bleeding.

Out of nowhere, I felt a hard tug on the leg of my overalls and heard the familiar, playful growl of my favorite talking dog. Trying to sit up, I used my elbows, and was almost there until Jeff jerked my leg so hard, I flopped back down on the ground as he shook the fabric of my pants with his teeth, yipping and snarling.

"Jeff! Knock it off!" I bellowed at him, yanking my leg back and lifting it high to avoid hitting the poor guy on the ground.

Clearly, Jeff didn't hear me, because he let go of the leg of my pants and went for my backside, sniffing and grunting, mimicking the behaviors of the dogs in the videos we'd shown him on YouTube so he could learn how to be an authentic canine.

As evidenced with his overzealous snorts, we were still a work in progress.

"Jeff!" I hissed, huffing a breath. "Staaahhp!"

Immediately, he backed off, sniffing his way toward me with his wet nose until his muzzle was almost at my ear. "Ix-nay on the e-bay un-way ith-way the og-day?" he whispered in Pig Latin, one of his favorite forms of communication (like I said, he sometimes behaves as though he's twelve).

"You *are* an ogday! You can't be un-way with the og-day if you already are an og-day!" I whisper-yelled back. "Now, ock-knay it off-nay!"

"Trixie!" I heard Higgs shout from above me. "Jeff! Down, boy! Down!" Hands, strong and sure, slipped under my armpits, scooping me up off the ground and standing me upright, but my foot got caught in the straps of my purse, now around my ankles, and I stumbled, knocking into his tall frame.

He caught me as we careened into the front of the store, sandwiching me between the hard wall of his chest and the brick facade. We were so close, his cologne wafted to my nostrils.

Which was appealing in a laundry-fresh way, but whatever.

He looked down at me, his dark eyes searching mine as Jeff stood by his leg, panting. "You okay, Trixie? Are you hurt?" he asked, lifting a hand to brush away the hair stuck to my lips.

"She's okay. Him, not so much," Coop commented over Higgs's broad shoulder, pointing in the direction of the ground.

We dispersed instantly, me grabbing at the strap of my purse to secure it around my torso and over my shoulder again, and Higgs rushing to the injured man's side. We both fell to our knees simultaneously, Higgs pressing two fingers to the man's neck as I circled his beefy wrist and felt for a pulse, trying to keep my eyes from straying to all points southern.

Our eyes met and Higgs shook his head, creating a lump in my throat. The man was gone. Thus, I closed my eyes and sent up a prayer his soul would find safe passage to wherever he landed.

Knuckles stuck his head out the door and in a somber tone said, "Police are on their way, Trixie. I told them it wasn't an emergency. Am I right?"

Higgs nodded to Knuckles as I looked over my shoulder and mouthed a *thank you* to him before rising, pressing my stinging palm to my thigh, my brain whirring with the visual of the scene before me.

"Let me go get Jeff's leash and get him under control, I'll be right back," Higgs said, leaving me an opportunity to talk to Coop who stepped over the man to join me.

Spitting more of my hair from my mouth, I latched on to her upper arm and pulled her to a portion of the sidewalk away from Higgs's ears. My eyes wide in disbelief, I asked, "Coop! What the heck happened? This man is *dead*! Why did you spend all that time keeping me from going outside when he was lying on the ground, before finding out if he was injured?"

She blinked her gorgeously fringed eyes at me, her gaze blank. "I didn't know he was dead, Sister… Er, Trixie. I thought he was just resting. When he got off the bike, he was breathing pretty hard."

My eyes went wider and my mouth fell open. "Coop, how could you not see he was *dead*? Look at him. He's all twisted up like a pretzel with his eyes wide open! Nobody *rests* with their eyes open!"

As I pointed to the man, my eyes strayed to the position of his body after I'd tripped over him. He was partially on his side, one arm tucked under him while the other sprawled out on the pavement.

One leg curved almost unnaturally behind him and the other was bent at the knee, supporting his bulky but muscled body. He wore a neon-orange pair of flip-flops, still on his feet, and an ID bracelet I couldn't quite see.

Coop placed her hands on her hips and lifted her chin. "I'm telling you the truth, Trixie. I saw him ride up on his bike and get off. Then he sat down. I thought he was just tired from the ride, so I didn't check to see if he was all right because he was sitting upright when I last looked. That's when you wanted to go get coffee for Knuckles, but I didn't want your tender eyes to see the naked man in front of our door. So I kept you from leaving the shop. That's why I told you to close your eyes. But I promise you, he was very much alive when I last looked at him."

Okay, in Coop's black and white take on things, I suppose her explanation made sense in the most rudimentary of ways. She wanted to protect me from naked men.

That seemed to be a concern for everyone. Nuns have seen naked bodies before, you know.

But forget the naked body. Something else occurred to me. "You do realize the police are going to be here any second, right? And that you have to keep your head on straight and tell them the absolute truth?"

Coop nodded. "I am always truthful."

I inhaled and tried to keep my eyes off the body, but it felt like he was everywhere. Maybe that was just because he was naked. Yet, I couldn't see anything but him, lying on the ground half on his side, his eyes glassy.

"Are you sure you didn't see anything else? He didn't look like he was in distress when he got off his bike?"

Coop crossed her arms over her chest and shook her head. "He didn't look like he was in distress. His cheeks were very red, but I figured he was just over-heated from riding his bike."

The sound of sirens blared their warning cry, cutting through the dusky purple of the evening as the sun prepared to set. "Are you okay, Coop? Will you be all right to talk to the police?"

This, after all, was the third dead body we'd happened upon in just a few short months. I wasn't sure if that was affecting Coop, because I couldn't tell *what* did or didn't affect her most of the time. Her stone face didn't lend to reading her emotions. I mostly had to go on instinct. But if some of the half stories she told me about Hell were true, she'd seen plenty of death.

"I'm fine, Trixie, but shouldn't you be taking pictures of the body? You know, like Stevie told us to do?"

Our mentor/ace crime solver, Stevie, had left an indelible impression on Coop, and to be frank, me, too. She'd taught us many things about a crime scene and was the one who'd sparked my interest in mysteries. But the real question—was this a crime scene? Did it warrant taking pictures?

Somehow, a naked dead body was very different than a clothed dead body. I felt a little dirty even considering taking pictures of this poor man when he was naked as a blue jay.

"Not every dead body is a murder victim, Coop.

Sometimes people die of natural causes," I said as I scanned the area around him.

Nothing surrounding him looked out of the ordinary other than the tire on his bike was a little crooked. Nothing at all. He'd dropped his bike down the sidewalk about couple of feet away, the red, white, and blue streamers shooting from the padded handles in a puddle on the ground right next to a green water bottle, resting in a divot in the pavement.

There was no blood. He didn't look at all injured. I couldn't see any marks on him from a weapon. Personally, I was leaning toward heart attack.

"I still think we should take pictures. Just in case," Coop remarked over her shoulder as she wandered off to see what Higgs, who'd returned with Jeff on his leash.

Suddenly, the police were on the scene, two patrol cars and one unmarked screeched to a halt at the curb. Detective Tansy Primrose hopped out of the driver's side of the unmarked car as the other officers leapt from theirs, yellow crime scene tape in their hands.

Tansy headed straight for us, her typically cheerful face zeroing in on mine. "Well, well, fancy who we have here. It's my favorite ex-nun turned killer wrangler. How are we, Miss Lavender? How's the foot?" she asked in her very proper British accent, but her tone was, as always, cheerful.

Since Fergus's murder, I'd seen Tansy around town at some of our favorite eateries and once at the local outdoor market, and I still liked her as much as I had upon our first meeting. I admired her drive, the fact that, according to Higgs, she'd fought her way up the ladder to make detective, and in the process, fought off some serious gender discrimination.

"This ex-nun and her foot are fine—finer than fine. You look well. How's you?"

She pulled out her small notepad from the pocket of her wrinkled blazer and winked. "I'm smashing. I see you've stepped in the middle of another dead chap. What say you, Trixie? Have you an expert opinion? Natural causes? Foul play?" she teased as her eyes roamed over the man on the ground only a few feet from me.

"I have no opinions, and even if I did, they wouldn't come with any sort of expertise. Unless you count watching *Death In Paradise*—a show I've been watching in your honor, by the way."

Gosh, I can't tell you how much I love a good British mystery. Stevie had turned me onto them, and since, I'd binge-watched more of them than I care to admit.

Now her eyes went playful but her tone was serious. "So are you telling me you don't know what happened here?"

"I didn't see anything. Not a thing. I just tripped over a dead guy on my way out to buy some coffee for the shop and some incoming clients. Swear."

"No theory to share, love?" she asked, a twinkle in her eye.

I gave her my best impish grin. I heard a little from

Higgs about what everyone was saying about the ex-nun who'd gone out of her way to solve a murder in order to move the investigation along so she could open her tattoo shop.

Tansy was enjoying teasing me, and I was going to let her because I liked her. "Nope. Not a one. I know my place, and it lies solely with a Netflix crime-show binge and a dream."

Tansy barked a laugh. "And what about your strange but wonderful friend, Coop? Did that unfairly gorgeous creature see anything?"

Coop came up behind the detective and tapped Tansy on the shoulder. "Strange but unfairly gorgeous creature is standing right here, Detective Tansy Primrose."

"Tans?" Higgs called out, tugging Jeff's leash to encourage him to walk. "Hey! Where ya been? I've texted you at least three times this week to see if you and Marv want to grab dinner."

She grinned at him, her blue eyes lighting up at the sight of her friend. "Sorry, bloke. It's been bloody madness at the station with two new detectives in training. Wee lads with nary any street experience, dumped on me as though I'm suddenly the precinct's answer to a uni dorm's house mother."

Higgs chuckled and nodded. "I remember the days. Still, work will always be there. You need to make time for yourself and the people who love you."

Tansy reached down and gave Jeff a stroke on the head. "Says the man who's out at three in the blessed morning, checking to be sure the homeless have enough blankets?"

He held up a hand and laughed. "Point made. But let's get together soon, okay?"

Tansy bobbed her bleached-blonde head, her chin-length hair swaying as she did. "Soon. I promise. Until then, did you see anything, Higgs?"

"Nope. I was late to supper. Didn't get here until after he was on the ground. But he's definitely dead. We checked."

Tansy's pencil-thin eyebrow rose, her face hesitant. "Have any thoughts on what might have occurred?"

"Nope," he said with a charming smile. Meaning, he didn't want any part of what had occurred.

"Good enough, love," she said with a return warm smile. Then she turned to Coop and drove her hand through the loop of her arm, taking her off in the other direction—standard procedure is usually to separate witnesses to garner the most authentic recollections. "Ready for a chat, darling?"

As I watched her corral Coop, I kept my fingers crossed my demon would do her civic duty to the best of her ability.

"So your assessment, Detective Lavender?" Higgs teased as he moved closer to me, Jeff's leash wrapped securely around his wrist.

Heat rushed to my cheeks. I was never going to live down the last time we'd found a dead body.

"You hush, ex-undercover police officer. I have no

assessments. As I told Tansy, I'm merely an innocent bystander who tripped over a dead man."

"Ah, but I see the gleam in your eye, Sister Trixie. It's the same one you had the night we did the stakeout under the Hawthorne. You love a good mystery to solve—it's evidenced by all the questions you ask me after watching endless episodes of *Psych*. There's no shame in your game."

"Do you mean the night I saved your hide, Cross Higglesworth, and nearly had my foot shot off?" I said on a giggle as we brushed shoulders.

Okay, a little honesty here. I didn't save-save his life. I happened upon the killer, who *happened* to shoot me by mistake while in a struggle with Higgs for the gun.

But Higgs wasn't at all daunted by the notion. One of the traits I admired most about him was how humble he was. I didn't feel at all like I'd saved his life, but *he* did, and he said so often. He called me selfless. I reminded him I was more asinine and careless than I was selfless, but he wasn't picking up what I was laying down.

"That's the one I'm talking about. You were all sparkly-eyed and salivating while we looked for a killer that night."

"I did not salivate, thank you very much. And I ask questions about *Psych* because I want to know if they're taking artistic license with the law and whether any of the facts about the forensics and procedures are real. I'm just getting my head screwed on right."

He peered down at me, the gleam in his eyes dancing. "Shawn and Gus take artistic license to a new level."

My eyebrow cocked upward. "You know who Shawn and Guster are? You watch *Psych?*"

"I might have watched an episode or forty."

I smiled up at him. It warmed my heart that he wasn't shunning everything remotely police-ish. I know Higgs suffers with the choices he made while he was undercover in a gang back in Minneapolis.

I also know those choices haunt him, and it's why he ultimately left undercover work to give service to his community in other ways. I only wish he'd open up about it more, but time was on my side. I hoped one day he'd feel comfortable enough to share with me.

"So what's *your* take on this?"

Instantly, Higgs clammed up, and I guess I couldn't blame him. He was clearly still raw, judging by the hardening of his jaw. "I have no take on anything."

Sighing, I lifted my face to the cool-ish breeze after the heat of the day and decided I wasn't going to pussy-foot around. I needed to know where I stood with Higgs as far as my interest in murder mysteries went.

"Listen, Higgs. I'm going to be brutally honest here."

"I'd expect nothing less from a nun."

"*Ex*-nun...and good. Because here it comes. I get that you want nothing to do with your former life. But if my asking questions and theorizing out loud about whatever—a murder-mystery show, a news story—upsets you, if it makes you feel like I'm pressuring you to join the conversation, say the word and I'll stop.

"I'm not asking you questions so that you'll suddenly realize you miss being an officer of the law. I'm not looking for epiphanies. This isn't me using my powers as a person of service to therapy you out of this thing you have about leaving the past behind. That's your choice, and I respect it. I'm just muttering out loud most times—it's obvious I don't know my backside from my elbow. But what I *won't* do is find out I'm driving you crazy with my murder chatter too late in the game. If you want to avoid all things murdery, say the word and I'll keep my thoughts to myself."

He paused a moment, his tanned face pensive as he looked off into the distance, where muffled laughter threaded its way to my ears—likely another batch of bikers.

He spoke after he swallowed, his Adam's apple bobbing up and down in his throat. "How can we be friends if I put the kibosh on your enthusiasm? I remember what it was like to be just as enthusiastic, even though a dead body is hardly something one should be enthusiastic about. But I remember the tingle in my gut, the itch to solve a crime. In fact, I remember it well."

"You still haven't answered my question. Would you prefer I leave that our taboo subject?"

"No," he said with an easy smile—a Higgs specialty, by the way. When things got uncomfortable, he smiled. "Theorize away, Sister Trixie. I'm all ears."

Avoid, avoid, avoid. But that was okay. As long as he wasn't silently grudging or angry that I couldn't shut up about my love of mysteries in general, especially a murder mystery, I was willing to let go until he was willing to let me in.

I'm not so sure *why* I wanted him to confide in me so much. Maybe it was because my nature is to nurture —to heal—but it meant something to me. And I had the feeling Higgs being able to confide in someone meant something to *him*, and he wouldn't do it without feeling one hundred percent comfortable.

Cracking my knuckles, I decided to indulge my whim. "Okay, Coop said he got off the bike and sat down and that was the last she saw of him, until I tripped over his body. So he was alive when he first got here."

He nodded his dark head. "And that leads you to believe what?"

Well, now that the expert had put me on the spot, I felt a little self-conscious… "Heart attack?"

"It could be a lot of things, and sure, a heart attack is certainly one of those things. But it doesn't hurt to think outside the box."

I peered at the naked man again, still seeing nothing out of the ordinary. "Kidney failure? Poisoning? Demonic possession?"

I can't believe I said that, but it just slipped out.

"Demonic possession?" he asked, wide-eyed, a half smile on his lips.

"Well, you said think outside the box…"

"I said think outside the box, not consider things that don't exist."

Says you...

I crossed my arms over my chest, tucking a hand under the strap of my purse. "Demonic possession *is* outside the box," I replied coquettishly.

Higgs popped his lips and grinned. "It's more like crushing the box. Next theory, please?"

"Lady Lavender!" a familiar voice yelled, forcing me to turn around and peer into the twilight. "Lady Lavender! Is that you?"

"Solomon?" I called out, just as he came into view, the oncoming darkness revealing the outline of his beloved shopping cart, filled to the brim with his most prized possessions.

After our run-in with Fergus's killer, Solomon had escaped the hospital once he was well enough to slip through the nurses' fingers. There was nothing he despised more than doctors, and hospitals, and tests.

But we'd gleaned a vague diagnosis for his behavior —nothing official, mind you; the doctors wouldn't cop to anything of the sort without thorough testing. However, the general consensus was that he was autistic, high-functioning to be precise, and that made perfect sense to Higgs and me.

As such, I'd spent some time online perusing autism sites, reading about the plights of parents with autistic children, trying to understand how I could best obtain Solomon's trust without frightening him off. I wanted him to know he could always turn to me—no matter the circumstance.

He sought me out often these days, always with his medieval shtick, which I'd come to learn was his most comfortable form of communication. He stuttered less, repeated words and phrases less if he had his Viking hat on and his fingers wrapped around the handle of his shopping cart—essentially, they were his safe items, rather like a child with his favorite blanket.

And that was okay by me. Solomon, despite his fears, was a sweet soul who'd picked (okay, stolen from the flower pots outside of the little burger place down the way, but whatever) flowers every day for me when my foot was mending, living in a body riddled with anxieties I was only just beginning to understand.

My ultimate goal was to have him see a doctor regularly, but that was a long way off. That he was seeking me out right now was enough.

As he rushed toward me, the wheels of his shopping cart clacking over the bumpy pavement, his Viking hat crooked atop his head, he called out again, "Lady Lavender! I must speak with you—'tis a matter of dire urgency!"

Putting a welcoming smile on my face, I waved him toward us. "My liege! What a wonderful surprise. How art thou this fine eve?"

He came to a full stop a couple of feet away from us, the distance he typically deemed comfortable between himself and another human being. "Terrible, Lady Lavender! Terrible, terrible, awful!" he crowed, his eyes darting from place to place but never quite landing on my face.

His hands, fingers splayed, were fluttering about his head, which meant he was stressed, and his gaunt face —fuller now that he knew he could come to me for a meal at least once a day—had lines of worry.

"Saulie? What's wrong, buddy?" Higgs asked, his tone laced with concern.

"No!" Solomon shouted abruptly. "No-no-no-no-no! You must not address me as such, you peasant!"

I patted Higgs on the arm and gave him the look, reminding him he wasn't playing the game.

Clearing his throat, Higgs corrected himself. "My apologies, oh great and wise king. How can we help you? Are you hungry, sire? Have you supped?"

My heart clenched in my chest at his words. Higgs's willingness to do whatever he could in order to earn Solomon's trust endeared him to me in ways I can't quite describe.

But Solomon made a face, his lips creating a thin line as he danced back and forth on the sneakers we'd bought him, and I found myself relieved to see he hadn't sold them for candy. Gobstoppers being his favorite.

"Whatever is the matter, King Solomon?" I pressed, my concern growing.

"*Him!*" he bellowed, pointing to the man on the ground, where two police officers stood guard.

My eyes widened, and I had to force myself not to

move closer to Solomon and latch on to his thin arm so he wouldn't escape me. "What about him, my liege?"

"They slaughtered him, Lady Lavender!" The words shot from his mouth like a cannonball, clearly with much effort. "Just like the warrior Braveheart! I saw with mine own two eyes! They killed him!"

My mouth fell open at Solomon's words.

But the only thing I could think was, dang it all, Coop had been right.

I should have taken pictures.

CHAPTER 4

*A*nd then I was so ashamed. Maybe that was morbid, and I was disgusted with myself for even thinking such, but darned if that tingle of the possibility of a crime didn't settle right in the pit of my belly, and I wasn't sure how I should feel about that.

Also, I hated to admit this, and I know Solomon's words sound very dramatic and maybe even a little crazy, but this wouldn't be the first time he'd rattled off some half-cocked story that, in the end, was true.

The hard part was parsing the fiction from the real story and connecting the dots. They didn't always add up. His recounting of events was always a riddle.

"Sire? Whatever doth thouest mean?" Higgs asked with clear concern, moving a little closer to Solomon while Jeff dug his heels in and strained against the leash.

Jeff was a little hesitant around Solomon, and with good reason. He'd once attempted to steal some turkey jerky right out of Solomon's pocket. He'd chased Jeff up and down the block, hurling soda cans at him and calling him thief.

"*Thouest?* Nice, Sir Higglesworth. It's thou. Whatever *dost thou* mean," I whispered to him, fighting a giggle.

But Solomon was already creating more space between himself and Higgs by dancing back and forth along the street in an erratic pattern. "Stay there, you scoundrel! Don't come any closer or I shall use my sword!"

Sword? Whoa, whoa, whoa. Had he somehow managed to find a sword? Cheese and rice, a sword in the mix was the last thing we needed.

But then Solomon pulled a large tree branch out of his beloved shopping cart and pointed it at Higgs, affecting the stance of a fencer ready to do battle.

Higgs instantly acquiesced and held up his hands in surrender.

"Okay, okay, King Solomon. I apologize. I'm only trying to help."

"You stay there, heathen!" he shouted, jousting an imaginary foe with the branch, his hat sliding around his head. "Only Lady Lavender can help me!"

It was time I stepped in. I took a tentative step forward, only enough so I could see Solomon's face clearer, yet not invade his space. "My liege? Can you tell me of your adventures this night? I wait with bated breath."

"Nice," Higgs whispered under his breath, making me preen a little.

Not full-on preen, mind you. Just a small preen. I mean, he's an expert on all things homeless, complimenting a total novice. That was worthy of a preen, don't you think?

"Him!" Solomon finally sputtered. "They murdered him with a steed of steel! That's what they did. They did, they did, they diiiid!"

I inhaled sharply and fisted my hands together. If what Solomon was saying was true, he'd seen this man murdered. But Solomon was hardly a reliable source. Yes, it was true he'd witnessed Fergus's murder, but his story of the events had been riddled with misleading information, and it was only through a series of revelations by Higgs that we put two and two together. As I said, what he told us had all been true, but it had been in the form of a brainteaser that, at the time, I didn't understand.

And what the heck did a steed of steel mean? But then a shiver slithered up my spine and it hit me, I think I knew what he meant. So, as I prepared to ask him my next question, I tried to keep the excitement of revelation out of my voice and remain calm and soothing.

"King, this steed of steel? Might I ask, dost thou mean a motor vehicle?"

"*Boom-booom!*" he bellowed, loud and raspy, his voice echoing along the street as he waved his pretend sword to and fro.

There was that tingle again. The one that said I was on to something. "So, are you saying someone hit him with the steed made of steel, my liege?" I asked, as I heard voices coming closer from the other end of the street.

"Is that what this fine chap's saying?" Tansy asked from behind us, her detective mode in full throttle, startling me with her sudden appearance.

However, the moment Solomon saw her, he instantly began to retreat, throwing his branch into the shopping cart and gripping the handles—which was unfortunate.

No matter how many times we'd tried to explain to him that the police only wanted to help in most cases, he simply couldn't hear us, leading me to believe he'd had a bad experience with law enforcement at one point in his life. If I hoped to find out what that was, it meant time and patience.

Solomon began to wave his finger in Tansy's direction with short jabs to the air.

Translation: he felt threatened.

"No, no, no! You stay away from me, copper! You're never gonna lock me up! Hear me? Never ever!" he yelped, latching on to the handle of his shopping cart and giving it a hard shove before he began to disappear into the darkness, off to wherever it was Solomon spent his nights.

Tansy's sigh was raspy and loud; she was clearly aggravated by Solomon's attitude toward her. "You do realize we'll need to question him after what he said, don't you, love?" she asked me, her eyes gleaming in the dark.

I nodded solemnly, knowing how much Solomon was going to hate that. "I do. Do you mind if I'm with him when you do? He's terrified of anyone with any authority to take him from the streets. He has no one to advocate for him, and I don't want him so frightened he'll run off on us again."

"Trixie's right, Tans. Solomon has a penchant for disappearing and forgetting his health in favor of his fears," Higgs agreed.

"Well, I'm no bloody monster. Of course you can be there, but he's not in any trouble. I promise not to use my interrogation tactics on him. No pulling his fingernails off one by one. I give you my word on the Queen's life."

I giggled then placed a hand on her arm to reassure her. "I don't mean to imply you'd ever hurt him, Tansy. I know you wouldn't intentionally upset him. But Solomon's easily spooked. Higgs is as sweet as pie to him, and he still thinks he's going to lock him in the storage closet at the shelter."

Higgs reached down and ran a hand over Jeff's ears. "She's right. I've known him much longer than Trixie, but he's bonded with her in a way I can't seem to achieve. He trusts her as much as he *can* trust. It'll be hard enough for you to bring him in for questioning, but to put him in an interrogation room will only agitate him, and you'll never get what you need then."

Tansy looked at us both and smiled. "Is there any particular way to bribe him? Money? Food, perhaps?"

"Gobstoppers," we said simultaneously, making Tansy laugh.

"Then Gobstoppers it is. You have my word I'll let you know when I'm ready to question him. I'll send Officer Meadows over for details on Solomon. Now, I must talk to your neighbor across the way and find out if he saw anything."

She meant Cyrus Fairmont, who owned a small market across the street. Cyrus was sweet and gentle and about eighty, and he refused to retire, according to his two sons, who both worked with him.

As Tansy went off to speak to a curious, okay nosy, Cyrus, who stood just beyond the threshold of Inkerbelle's, one of the officers standing watch over the body approached us. If my estimation was correct, he was easily over six feet and lanky, and probably no older than twenty-five. He had reddish-brown hair, cut short and slicked back on the sides, with a thatch left longish on top that had a penchant for falling over his forehead.

He sidled up to me, his casual stance and easygoing expression making me comfortable. "Miss Lavender?"

I smiled up at him, pushing my hands into the pockets of my overalls. "That's me. How can I help you?"

"Oh, I know who you are," he assured in a warm tone.

I pursed my lips and cocked my head. "You know me? Have we met?"

He grinned, flashing a set of exceptionally white teeth that were almost perfect but for his incisor, which overlapped the tooth to the right. "No, ma'am. I should say, I know *of* you. You're a legend around the station."

"Legend?"

"Yes, ma'am. You're the ex-nun who saved Higgs's butt. We talked about it at the station for days. I'm Oziah Meadows, by the way, but everybody calls me Oz. I hope you'll do the same." He held out a hand, which I took, a little taken aback by the word "legend."

Higgs slapped him on the back good-naturedly. "Quit perpetuating the myth, huh? I mean, whose side are you on, anyway?" he joked as Oz reached down and stroked Jeff's head.

Putting my arms behind my back, I cracked my knuckles, leaned into Higgs and taunted, "Hear that, ex-undercover police officer, I'm *legend*."

"And super humble," Higgs replied on a laugh.

Oz chuckled, his pen hovering over his notepad. "Anyway, I need to get some information on your friend Solomon for Detective Primrose. Maybe the places he frequents—for future reference and availability when he's questioned. And she wanted me to reassure you once more, she won't do anything without you there with him."

His words warmed my heart. If only I could get Solomon to trust Tansy the way I did. "You sure can.

Whatever you need, I'm happy to help. And just call me Trixie, please."

The moment Oz opened his mouth, we heard someone cry out in the dark, "Agnar? Agnar, where are you?" The voice was definitely male and strained, rife with worry.

Both Higgs and I looked at one another. "Agnar?" I repeated—and then realized they were probably referring to the dead man. "I think we've found who our dead guy belongs to."

"What makes you think *he's* Agnar?" Higgs asked, pushing a hand into the pocket of his jeans, his brow furrowed.

"He's blond."

Higgs's brow furrowed. "Meaning?"

"His name is Scandinavian or maybe Swedish— definitely something Nordic."

"I don't get it. Where are you going with that tidbit? Take me with you down this path of supposition. How could you possibly know that, because he's blond, he's Scandinavian and he's this Agnar? " he asked.

"Because he's blond."

"Still feeling a little left out, Sister Trixie. Care to explain?"

"Most people from a Nordic country are blond —*really* blond—like the dead guy. He's that white blond. You know, like that supermodel. Um… Elin Nordegren. You know who I mean. She was married to Tiger Woods, the golfer."

"You watch golf?"

Yes. We'd watched golf at the convent, as crazy as that sounds. We have all the amenities everyone else does, like cable TV. We just don't use them very often simply due to the fact that we're too tied up with service to our community.

But everyone needs to de-stress. We did it by watching golf, and we'd loved Tiger Woods, until he did the unthinkable and stepped out on his marriage to the gorgeous Elin. Oh, the uproar that had caused around the convent—and then we'd prayed for his salvation. We didn't think Sister Catherine Grace, who we were convinced had a crush on Tiger, would ever be the same.

"You'd be surprised what nuns do. We need down-time, too, *and* we shower without our clothes on. Crazy, right?"

"I don't ever want to think about a nun without her clothes on. It's unthinkable. But I'll say it again, you're not like any nun I've ever known, Trixie Lavender."

I barked a laugh and squinted my eyes in the direction the voices were coming from.

Higgs nudged my shoulder with his. "So anyway, what does all that have to do with the dead guy?"

"Like I said, he's blond—very blond—and his name is probably Agnar. Agnar is certainly Nordic."

Higgs bounced his head and smiled in under-standing as he stuck out his fist for a bump. "*Nice*, Sister Trixie. Well done, if you're right."

I *was* right. I knew I was right, and while I was busy being right, I was trying not to preen some more, but my cheeks wouldn't have it. They were beet red and hot.

Coop appeared from wherever she'd been, reminding me we had a dead body on our hands and as the voices grew louder, calling out Agnar's name, I worried these people belonged to this man, and they'd see him crumpled on the sidewalk, at his most vulnerable.

"Officer Meadows? Can we cover him up? I'm afraid this batch of bikers might belong to the dead man. I'd hate for them to see him like that."

He peered down at me and smiled gently, but shook his head. "I'm afraid we can't. Not until forensics clears the scene. But my partner and I can stand in front of him, if that helps."

I patted him on the arm and smiled my gratitude. "It does. You're a prince among men, Officer Meadows. Thank you."

"Oz, please, ma'am. Just call me Oz."

"Only if you'll stop calling me ma'am," I joked, and he laughed as he went to stand in front of the dead man, his likeability factor ratcheting up ten notches.

"Agnar? Answer me, my man!" a man yelled, getting closer all the time.

"Coop? Maybe we should get some blankets. Do we have any here at the shop? I'm betting these people are looking for the dead man. I'm also betting they're as naked as him. That might be uncomfortable in light of the situation."

Higgs held up some keys. "Blankets are in the storage closet, Coop. Grab them, would you please?"

She nodded, and he lobbed the keys to her, leaving us to face the music as the bikers came into view.

"You ready?" Higgs asked, his fingers brushing mine, concern in his voice.

Were you ever ready to see the reaction of someone after finding out their loved one had passed? I've seen it many times, but it never gets any easier. Yet, I nodded firmly, the sorrow of what was to come, weighing heavy on my heart. "I'm ready."

The first of the small cluster of riders to come to a skidding halt was a tall, reed-thin man with dark hair and a moustache.

He didn't say a word. He simply hopped off his bike, his flip-flops clapping along the pavement until he came to a full stop at Oz and his partner.

"Agnar?" he whispered into the night, a raw, hoarse sound emitting from his throat as he peered around the police officers.

"Do you know this man?" I asked, as Coop stealthily approached with a blanket she threw over his shoulders and tucked around his neck as though he were a child.

His hands reached for the blanket almost the same time he let out a sob of pain. "Yes…" he said, then cleared his throat as his eyes welled with tears. "Yes. He's my best friend."

Oh, how dreadful. Instantly, my throat tightened

up, but Higgs stepped in like a true champ while Tansy was still busy with Cyrus.

"I'm Cross Higglesworth, and this is Trixie Lavender. Your name is, sir?"

"Myer. Myer Blackmoore," he muttered as his eyes appeared to finally focus on Higgs.

"Please, come sit down and maybe we can talk until the detective comes to officially question you?" I asked, latching on to his rail-thin arm, leading him to the small table and chairs we had just outside the shop's doors.

Myer stiffened and shrank against my touch, halting his steps. "Wait! We have to cut Suzanne off at the pass! She'll be here any second. She wasn't that far behind me—she's with the rest of our friends. Oh, no. No, no, no!" he wailed. "She can't see him like this! This will kill her!"

"Agnar? Myer?" a husky, sultry voice called, emerging from the dark. "Myer? What's going on? Talk to me, please!"

A coppery redhead with wild, curly hair and nothing but her birthday suit on ground to a halt on her ten-speed bike, her alabaster skin glowing in the dark, lit up by our neon Inkerbelle's sign. This must be Suzanne.

She trembled as she approached us. "Myer? Where's Agnar?"

"Suzanne," he whispered, snaking a thin hand toward her, but she recoiled and shook her head, as though denying what she was seeing would make it all go away.

"*No!*" She hissed the word, putting her hand over her mouth, her fingers shaking. "No, Myer. Tell me that's not Agnar! Is he dead, Myer? *Is he dead?*"

Coop handed me a blanket I immediately flung over Suzanne's slender shoulders, wrapping my arm around her and tucking her close to me. "Suzanne? My name is Trixie Lavender. I own the shop you're standing in front of. Would you come with me so we can talk?"

I know I can get myself into some hot water for talking to someone before the police get their chance, but the ex-nun in me knows no legal boundaries. She was hurting. I wanted to comfort her. It's ingrained. The heck with the rules.

As she allowed me to guide her toward the chairs, Knuckles suddenly burst from the shop's door, his burly body rushing toward us.

"*Suzanne?* Is that you?"

"You know her?" I blurted my astonishment, feeling all manner of fool when I heard how insensitive my question sounded.

He nodded as though in a daze, his eyes wide, his jaw slack. "Suzanne's my ex-girlfriend."

CHAPTER 5

This very young woman was Knuckles's ex-girlfriend? She didn't look a day over thirty-five—tops. I didn't get it. Obviously, judging by the look on Higgs's face, he didn't get it, either.

I tried not to peer at her too closely as she stared at Knuckles, but if she was his age, she looked amazing for fifty-nine. Or maybe it was just the dim lighting of the street lamp. Either way—wowza.

Suzanne turned away from me then, her lean body graceful and fluid as her blue eyes widened. "Donald? Oh, Donnie, is that really you?" she asked, her voice squeaking in disbelief.

Knuckles, a.k.a. Donald P. Ledbetter, nodded, his face riddled with concern. He opened his beefy arms and she ran into them, collapsing against his bulky frame with a sob. "He's dead, Donnie! He's dead!" she cried in husky sobs.

As though reading my mind, Coop was there, a box

of tissues in hand, pulling the thin pieces of paper out and sliding them into Knuckles's fist for Suzanne.

He nodded his thanks, but he didn't speak a word as he shook Myer's hand and led Suzanne to the chairs, encouraging her to sit down. "C'mon, Susie-Q. Let's sit."

When she tried to get a glimpse of Agnar, Knuckles cupped her chin and turned her face toward him, blocking out her view of the corpse by rooting his big body in front of her much smaller frame.

"I'm going to take Jeff back to the shelter, but I'll be right back. You okay on your own, Sister Trixie?" Higgs asked with a supportive squeeze to my shoulder.

"I'll be fine." Reaching down, I gave Jeff a rub under the chin with a smile. "You be a good boy for Daddy, buddy, and no chewing up shoes. The men at the shelter need them. You can still be a dog and not leave everyone shoeless, mister."

In yet another failed effort to be one with the dog, Jeff had chewed up every shoe left at the foot of each shelter bed, leaving some very displeased residents. Boy, had that been some wakeup call.

Higgs left with Jeff while I continued to watch Knuckles with Suzanne. So calm and gentle, just like the sweet giant he is.

"I hear this is the victim's wife?" Tansy asked in a hushed whisper as she approached, and it was one of the things I liked best about her.

Despite the fact that she was an officer of the law first, she had a heart, and she would allow Suzanne her moment of shock and grief before she pounced with her questions. I'd seen her do it two weeks ago when one of our shop owner neighbors had a death in the family. She'd let them process finding their mother in the parking lot, dead in her car, before questioning them.

"Yes. She's Agnar's wife," Myer answered, his eyes glassy, his voice scratchy. "I don't understand what happened. We lost him a little ways back and we've been looking for him ever since. *Who* did this to him?"

"What makes you think someone did something to him?" I wondered out loud. My initial thought was he'd had a heart attack, but after talking to Solomon and now hearing Myer, I had to consider.

His reply was stilted, his eyes heavy with sorrow. "I don't know what made me say that. I…just…I just… assumed something happened. He's healthy and in great shape, and all of a sudden he's dead? It doesn't make any sense. No sense at all."

Tansy looked into his eyes, hers sharp and at the ready. "Would you come with me, Mr…?"

"Blackmoore. Myer Blackmoore," he murmured as though in a daze, following Tansy, his shoulders hunched.

Three more people on bikes came to a stop in front of the shop, exiting their bikes en masse and heading straight for Suzanne, who looked so fragile under the lights of our sign. They closed in on her, crowding Knuckles out.

Coop and I passed blankets around to them,

hovering outside the circle as they consoled their friend. I'd like to say I was altruistic enough not to eavesdrop, but that would be a lie. I was totally eaves-dropping. What Myer said had unsettled me and made me decide maybe Agnar hadn't died of anything natural at all.

Unfortunately, I was picking up very little in the way of evidence, and only some odds and ends of their conversation could be heard over Suzanne's sobbing anyway.

Turning to Knuckles, I grabbed his hand and held it tight. "Are you okay?"

He patted me on the arm and pulled me close to him. "I'm fine, Trixie girl. Just a little in shock. Haven't seen Susie-Q in at least twenty-years, and I sure didn't know she was friends with Myer."

I cocked my head and looked up at him. "You know him, too?"

"He's who I was talking about, Trixie. Him and his friends from LA. You know, the ones who were coming in for tats? That's him. He's a big-time chef turned entrepreneur. Has a bunch of restaurants all over the world."

Ugh. "Oh, Knuckles. I'm so sorry. I didn't know these were the people you meant…"

He pinched my cheek and smiled down at me. "How could you? But it's all right, kiddo. I'm more worried about them than anything else."

"So Suzanne's your ex-girlfriend? Where does she fit in with Candice?" That was his deceased wife, who he talked about with great frequency. If the stories Knuckles told us about Candice weren't exaggerations, we could all only hope to have the kind of love story they'd shared.

"I did have a life before her, you know," he said on a jovial chuckle. "I guess you don't think about things like that because you've only ever been a nun. Candice and me—we didn't get married until I was almost thirty-two, had my Gwennie a year later. Did a lot of livin' before that while I was making a name for myself as a tattoo artist. Suzanne's from my sordid past."

He was right. I guess I didn't know much about what it was like to have a life that wasn't cloistered. I'd just assumed he'd always been married to Candice, or it felt like that anyway.

Curiosity got the better of me, and I hoped he wouldn't be too upset by my next question. "Define sordid past," I teased, giving him a squeeze around his waist.

"She was twenty-one, and I was thirty. Met at a biker bar, had a wild fling, I broke it off and she went off to pursue her acting career. Which in LA means, she got a better offer. Probably from a big director."

My jaw unhinged. This beautiful creature with the alabaster skin and fiery red hair falling down her back looked amazing for her age—or maybe it was just the lighting. But even if that were true, her body—and she was naked, so it wasn't hard to see—was in primo shape.

"Wait. Are you telling me she's *fifty*? Shut the front door."

"Well, you know LA is the land of plastic surgery, kiddo. Seems like there isn't much they can't do these days. If you think she looks good now, shoulda seen her back in the day. But I gotta admit, she still looks pretty good."

I snorted and nudged him in the ribs. "I'll say."

He patted his belly. "'Course, I've put on forty pounds since the last time I saw her," he said in a tone that sounded quite self-conscious and totally unlike my Knuckles.

Was that regret I heard in my friend's voice? Embarrassment? I wouldn't have it. Knuckles is one of the finest men I've ever known.

"Forty pounds of love," I joked. "You're perfect the way you are, and I'll bet you my morning coffee for a week, she isn't nearly as kind as you are."

I paused for a moment, wondering about these people and their lives. I thought I sensed bitterness in Knuckles's voice when he talked about Suzanne.

"You're a sweet kid, Trixie. Always lookin' for the good in folks. It's what I like most about you. That and your crazy convent stories."

I chuckled and winked. "I don't have to look far with you, mister. So...these people...did you know Agnar or any of the others?"

Crossing his big arms over his barrel chest, he shook his head. "Nope. Just Myer. We go way back. Like I said, he's an entrepreneur—owns a bunch of restaurants all over the world, but his home base is LA."

"I'm so sorry this is happening, Knuckles."

"Me, too. For Suzanne. You know what happened to him yet?"

Shaking my head, I rocked back on my heels and tucked my hands into the bib of my overalls. "I'm not sure. At first I thought it was a heart attack, but if you listen to Solomon, he claims a car hit him. I think. I don't know. You know what Solomon's like. His stories are always a jumbled mess of a puzzle that needs putting together."

Despite the circumstances, Knuckles gave me a warm smile. "But he's a smart one, that guy. Smart as a whip—just a little quirky. I like quirky. Keeps me on my toes."

One of the traits I loved most about my buddy Knuckles was his ability to accept a situation at face value with no questions asked, as he did with Coop, and then Solomon. He didn't care that Solomon was way left of center, he accepted him and his quirks anyway.

Often, I'd find Knuckles bringing him leftovers from our dinners together the night before, or making sure he had a spare sandwich on hand in the shop just for Solomon.

"Solomon's a good guy, but I'll warn you, his story's pretty nutty." I explained what Solomon had told us about the steed of steel, which left me still shaking my head.

Knuckles let out a deep breath. "So you think he was hit by a car? He doesn't look like a car hit him. There's no blood. No marks on his body."

This made no sense. Solomon had made it sound like he was ranting about a car, but Knuckles was right. He didn't have any marks, suggesting a car had hit him.

"No, he sure doesn't. I'm not really sure what Solomon meant. Maybe he meant a bicycle? I mean, if you'll recall, he told me Fergus had been talking to someone about doing the laundry and it turned out, he was referring to money laundering. It could mean anything, but I won't know until I talk to him again."

As I watched Suzanne, crying uncontrollably while her friends rallied 'round, I thought of something else when Tansy parted the crowd and looked down at her, notepad and pen in hand. Something not so great that was sure to upset Knuckles.

Wincing, I asked, "You do realize the police always suspect the spouse first, right?"

He looked down at me and nodded. "Don't you think I hear you watching all those mysteries at night on your laptop out on your deck while ya sketch? Sure I know she'll be the likely suspect, but I'm not worried about it. Suzanne wouldn't hurt a fly. She was always a greedy one, hopping from guy to guy until she found the one with the biggest wallet—it's part of the reason we broke up way back. But that's no crime, Trixie girl. But kill someone? She was greedy, but she wasn't murderous. Besides, she was young and impulsive back in the day. With time comes wisdom, you know? She's probably a whole different person now. "

Relief flooded my veins for Knuckles and his friend. "Good to know. I just want you to be prepared. Speaking of preparation, maybe I should grab some water bottles for everyone?"

Knuckles chucked me under the chin. "You're a good egg, kiddo, but I got this. I'll go get some water and see what Lucy-Goosey is up to. He's probably hiding from all the drama out here and needs someone to talk him down. You do your nun thing. They look like they could use a sympathetic ear, and you sure are good at that. I'll be right back if Suzanne needs me."

He took his leave while I continued to hover around the fringe of their conversation. Slipping closer, but staying out of the streetlight, I tried to make myself seem available without appearing nosy.

There were three other people in their group besides Myer and Suzanne. Someone named Lucinda, a pretty brunette with chin-length hair and a heart-shaped face. An extremely handsome, chiseled guy named Edwin with the loveliest green-gray eyes I'd ever seen on a man, and still another gentleman who's name I hadn't quite caught, but was the largest of the bunch with a pot belly and a double chin.

Deciding I should see how I could help, I asked, "Is there anything I can get anyone? Are you all warm enough?"

Suzanne hopped up from her chair, not at all

concerned that her blanket had fallen to the ground as she rushed toward me. "This is your shop, right?"

I nodded, noting how wide her red-rimmed eyes were when she latched onto my hand. "It is, and I'm so sor—"

"Did you see *anything*? Notice anyone or even anything strange? The detective said you tripped over his body, for bloody sake! How could this have happened right under your nose? Are you blind or just a moron?"

Grief does strange things to people. Everyone handles the emotion in a different manner. Anger was a common reaction, so I wasn't at all upset with her harsh words. Rather, I patted her hand to console her and kept my tone even.

"I understand you're upset, Suzanne, and I'm happy to answer any questions you have about what happened. I didn't see anything, unfortunately, but of course, I'm so sorry for your loss and suffering."

Her face went from anguished anger to outrage in seconds as she snatched her hand away. "Suffering? *Suffering?* My husband is *dead* and you tripped over him like he was a bag of nothing more than trash, you idiot!" she howled at me, her pretty face a mask of pain.

"Suzanne!" her friend Lucinda reprimanded, placing a hand on her shoulder. "This was horrible, but it's not her fault she fell over him. He died right at the threshold of her store, for God's sake. We don't even know what happened to him yet. Stop before you say something you don't mean. Stop right now!"

The handsome man named Edwin stepped forward, tucking a blanket back around Suzanne with tender fingers. "Lucy's right, pretty. You're tired and upset, and with good reason, but this woman's hardly at fault," he soothed as he eyed me from head to toe with his gorgeous gaze.

"Always with the drama. No cameras around for your close-up today, Suzanne," the man whose name I hadn't heard muttered. He sounded as though this was something Suzanne did on a regular basis—make a big deal out of things, but I could hardly blame her. This *was* a big deal. Her husband was dead, after all.

"Hush, Grady!" Lucinda chastised in a whisper-yell, her pretty face wrapped in distaste. "How can you even say such a thing? Her husband's *dead*, you dolt. That's pretty dramatic. Now, if you're not going to help us, go away and keep your mouth shut. And cover," she waved a hand at his exposed southerly parts, "*that* up!"

I backed away, realizing Suzanne was in no state of mind to receive heartfelt condolences or any sort of counsel. I raised a hand and waved off their reprimands.

"Please, no explanations or apologies necessary. I'll just wait over there and if you need anything— anything at all, please don't hesitate. We're happy to help."

I made my way to where Coop stood, her stance relaxed, her hands in the pockets of her jeans, and as always, in silent, quiet observation. "She's not nice."

I blew out a breath of pent up air, letting my chest

expand with a cleansing release. "She's just upset, Coop. Her husband just died. It's to be expected. No worries."

Coop's eyes narrowed. "That's not what I mean at all."

My brow furrowed in confusion. "Then what do you mean?"

"I mean she's not a nice person. Her aura is all wrong."

"Her aura? Coop, I swear on all that fancy tattoo equipment in there, if you tell me you can see auras, I'm going to have *you* exorcised."

Of course I was teasing, but listen, she *was* a demon after all. She has admitted to knowing things I never dreamed possible. Seeing auras isn't so far out of the realm of possibility.

She pursed her lips, her eyes catching the light of the streetlamp, making them sparkle. "You know, Trixie Lavender, I've been thinking about exactly that. Maybe an exorcism is what you need? You certainly know people who can help. I'm sure not everyone at the convent is angry with you. Maybe we should call them and ask if they'll perform one?"

My breath caught in my throat. I'd thought the same thing, too. But who would believe me? Who would believe my horrifying behavior was a real, honest-to-goodness possession?

A true exorcism is very rare. Typically, the person declared possessed is mentally ill, or so I've read, and medication is almost always the suggested route to start any investigation of possession.

The very last resort is a real exorcism like the ones you see in movies, and they've been wildly exaggerated by Hollywood. Still, it's something I've often given thought to as a way to figure out what's inside me and why, but I won't lie and tell you it doesn't scare the pants off me.

I bent my knee, placing the sole of my foot up against the brick of our building. My foot still ached from time to time since the bullet wound, especially if I was on my feet for too long, and stretching eased the ache.

"Maybe what I need is to help these people in this moment and worry about me later. So explain the aura thing to me. Are you serious? Can you really read them?"

Coop shrugged in her unaffected manner, her slender shoulders rising and falling. "It's not really something you see, and if someone tells you otherwise, you tell them they're full of baloney and cheese. It's more a vibration, and Suzanne's vibration isn't a nice one. She radiates mean."

"Well, maybe she's just having a bad aura day. I mean, her husband's dead, Coop."

"It's not like hair, Trixie. You can't have a bad aura day. You either have a bad aura or you don't."

I'm almost afraid to ask about my aura…

I sighed into the night, fighting a yawn. It had been a

long day full of very strange things. "Well, then, okey-doke. Auras aside, maybe she isn't a nice person whether her husband's dead or not, but she still deserves our sympathy and respect in a time so dire. So let's put our best foot forward and see how we can help."

"You're a good person, Trixie. That lady was unkind to you and you continue to be kind despite her poor behavior. You are the epitome of do unto others."

I blushed and waved her and her Bible quote off. I hadn't opened the good book in months, and some-times I felt dreadfully guilty about that. As though I'd turned my back on the one thing that had cared and nurtured me for so long. But then I remembered it was also the one thing that had condemned me forever.

Besides, I didn't necessarily believe the Bible and its teachings hadn't been misinterpreted—after all, humans had translated its teachings. My goal nowa-days is less radical, far simpler.

I want to be the best person I know how to be. It's all I can offer after losing everything, and I guess some scripture figures into that. I want everyone to believe in what they want to believe in, as long as the end result is a mentally healthy outcome.

Still, I was curious about what Coop had learned. "So tell me, Coop, what do you know about do unto others?"

"I've been reading the Bible and learning verses in order to better understand you and why you devoted your life to an unseen, unheard entity."

Huh. I'd never thought of it like that before, but in

its simplest form, it was true. I had handed my life over on pure faith—sight unseen—which probably comes off a little nuts when you strip down the act.

"Then I guess that makes you a good person, too, Coop DeVille."

"Why?"

I reached over and squeezed her shoulder. "Because you're interested in something other than yourself. That shows true selflessness. I'm proud of you."

"Am I still selfless if I want to slice that mean Suzanne's head off because she was so rude to you?"

I wrinkled my nose. "The slicing of heads is definitely not a good thing, but your motivation for it is spot on. How about we leave it at that?"

"I'm happy to leave it at that because it means I don't have to doubt my wish to become like everyone else."

I looked over at her as she leaned against the brick with me, pressing her back against the hard surface. "Never doubt you're a good person, Coop. *Never.*"

She pulled her phone from her pocket, holding it up. "I think people are at least starting to notice I'm trying to be a good person."

"What do you mean?" I asked as she held the phone closer to my face. I cocked my head as I looked at her phone, and saw Edwin's name (his last name being Garvey, BTW) and number on the screen—as in, Edwin the man who was in the height of consoling Suzanne.

"While you were talking to Knuckles, that man over there put his phone number into my phone and called me honey. I don't think he'd do that unless he thought I was a good person, do you?"

I couldn't help it, I burst out laughing.

Oh, my sweet demon.

So many lessons, so little time.

CHAPTER 6

"Knuckles? Are you all right? Please be all right. I won't sleep if you're unwell emotionally. I'd hate it if you're sad," Coop said as we all sat together in the shop, decompressing after our incredibly tense night. She busied herself pouring us some coffee and in general, fretting over Knuckles.

While Coop fretted openly, I fret internally. Knuckles had been in a vulnerable space these last weeks. His emotions were likely heightened and exacerbated by seeing an old flame and it was showing up in his posture and the pained expression on his face.

Everyone had cleared out now. The bikers were off at the police station being questioned by Tansy and her team, but not before Suzanne had made a sobbing plea for Knuckles to help her find out what happened to Agnar.

And it had torn him up as she'd clung to him and

cried, until her friend Lucinda had to pry her off Knuckles.

His normally cheerful face and jovial attitude were all dried up as he fretted over his well-preserved ex-girlfriend. But he lifted his mug and tipped it at Coop in gratitude. "I'm all right, Coop. Just a little worried about Suzanne."

Goose slapped him on his broad back with a long-fingered hand. "She was always one for the drama, Knuck. I know her husband's dead, but she really ramped up the carrying on. Funny how it was only when you were lookin.'"

What an interesting observation, one I hadn't noticed and wished now I'd given more attention.

"You knew Suzanne, too, Goose?" I asked, pulling my stool closer to the small area we had set up for clients with a couch and tables, where everyone had gathered.

This was the second person who had dubbed her dramatic, making me wonder why she felt dramatics were necessary. Her husband had died. That was plenty dramatic, but of course, I didn't know her the way these two did.

Goose nodded, running a hand over the black do-rag with the skulls on it that covered his balding head, his craggy face screwed up in distaste. "We all knew Suzanne. She hung around for about a year or so before she moved on to greener pastures—and that's *exactly* what that girl did. Can't tell me otherwise."

Knuckles hitched his jaw at Goose, squinting one eye. "It wasn't like that, Goose. I broke up with her."

Goose sipped his coffee and nodded his head, the wrinkles on his cheeks deepening as he grimaced. "Yeah, you did. After ya found out she was foolin' around with somebody else. You didn't believe any of us at first. She did ya wrong, pal—didn't like it way back when, don't like it now. You still can't see her for what she is, can ya?" he asked in his hushed tone.

Since we'd hired Goose, he hadn't been much of a communicator. He was quiet and quick about everything he did. That he was speaking up meant something. The more I got to know him, the more I got the feeling he didn't talk unless he had something important or meaningful to say.

Knuckles shrugged his wide shoulders as Coop patted him on the back with an awkward thump of her hand. "Water under the bridge. Long since over. She was young, Goose. I think we all have a story or two about the stupid things we did at that age—especially you, buddy. And if you ask me, *I* moved on to greener pastures, because breaking up with Suzanne led me to my Candice."

Coop was immediately interested, her face open and curious. "I love Candice stories, Knuckles. So-so much. They make me happy because she made *you* happy. I like it best when you're happy."

Knuckles gave her a brief smile, reaching up to chuck her under the chin. "I'm glad to hear that, Coop. I'd hate to think all my babbling bores you two."

We loved to hear about his late wife and all the wonderful things they'd done together. He told us stories over dinner or when something on TV reminded him of her. They'd been so happy; Knuckles had been so happy that sometimes his recollection of that joy made my breath catch in my throat.

"Then maybe you should think of Candice tonight, Knuckles," Coop suggested, curling up on the sofa next to him and patting him on his tattooed arm. "Then you won't be so sad."

If only it were that easy. Maybe for Coop it *was* that easy, but I could see Knuckles struggling with an emotion I wasn't even sure he understood.

He ran a hand over his beard before he reached over to the arm of the couch and stroked Livingston, who allowed Knuckles to pet him and only complained about it when we were alone, in the confines of our own space.

"I'm not sad in the way you think, Coopie. I'm sad something bad happened. You know, like when you hear about someone dying tragically on the news, but you don't know them—it makes you sad, right?"

Coop looked like a deer in the headlights, unsure how to answer. She didn't differentiate feelings the way we all do—to date; it was black and white with her. Her eyes went to my face, looking for answers, gauging my reaction.

So I stepped in, nodding my head in understanding. "Yeah. Like the story about the little girl who was lost up on the trails at Mt. Hood, remember that, Coop? We didn't know her, but when we heard what happened, we were sad that she was probably alone and frightened in the woods."

Coop nodded vigorously. "But they found her safe and sound with her dog. That was nice. Very nice."

"Yes, it was. But that's the kind of sad Knuckles means. Sadness sometimes has degrees."

"It sure do," Goose commented, reaching over and ruffling Coop's hair with his slender fingers.

A knock on the glass made us all turn around to see Higgs at the door. He'd promised Knuckles he'd use his connections at the Cobbler Cove precinct to find out what was happening with Suzanne and the rest of her friends. I hoped he had something to brighten Knuckles night.

I jumped up to let him in, letting Jeff burst through the door and hop up into Coop's lap, where he settled with a contented sigh. He might struggle with being one with the dog, but he had the lap sitting down pat.

"Hey, guys," he said as I grabbed him a stool and motioned for him to sit. "Knuckles? How ya feelin'?"

"How's Suzanne?" he asked, pushing himself to the edge of the cushion.

Higgs's lips went thin as he took a deep breath and looked at Knuckles, his brow furrowing. "I think 'emotional' is the word best used to describe her right now, but physically, she's fine. She's in good hands, Knuckles. I promise Tansy will be gentle."

I was still learning about Higgs, and two of the things I paid particular attention to were his facial expressions and tone of voice. His tone of voice said he was choosing his words carefully so as not to offend Knuckles. Meaning, Suzanne was maybe overdoing the grieving widow act.

Goose cackled softly, slapping his jean-clad thigh. "Told ya. Milkin' it for all it's worth is what she's doin', the little viper. Always the actress."

Knuckles let out a breath that sounded like he'd been holding it in forever. "Look here, Goose, let it be, okay? That was well over twenty-something years ago. Maybe she's changed. People grow up. They mature. Back then she was just a kid—an impulsive, selfish kid. But we all grow up. So look here, the woman lost her husband. She has every right to milk the situation. That's the end of it. I don't want to hear any more of your nonsense."

So obviously, something more than just a breakup had occurred between Suzanne and our Knuckles. He'd made it sound very casual, but Goose certainly saw it quite differently, and it rubbed Knuckles the wrong way.

Goose lifted his hands in the air in surrender, but his eyes said he was worried for his longtime friend. "Fine by me. Just remember how she tore your guts up is all I'm sayin'. And now, out of respect for you and your wishes, I won't say no more." He sat back in his chair and sipped his coffee, zipping his lip as promised.

"So have we heard any preliminary findings on how Agnar died, Higgs?" I asked, hoping to diffuse the tension between Goose and Knuckles.

Higgs scrolled his phone, probably for a text from his friend at the station. "Nothing official, mind you, but talk is either a heart attack as you suggested or maybe internal injuries."

I jabbed a finger in the air. "I'd bet that's what Solomon meant! I bet he was hit by a car," I reasoned. That felt right. I don't know why, but the words coming from my mouth felt right.

Higgs nodded. "You could be right, but word is no one made mention of it if it happened. No one from the group, that is."

I pursed my lips and leaned forward, putting my elbows on my knees. "How far ahead could he have been that they missed him being hit by a car? And if a car hit him, how the heck was he still riding his bike by the time he got here with nary a mark on him to be found? Coop said he got off the bike and sat down. And how did a car get in the mix anyway? There weren't supposed to be any cars on the Naked Bike Ride route, if I recall correctly."

The corner of Higgs's mouth lifted in a half smile. "That's why it's called a hit and run or a criminal act. *If* that's even what happened. We don't know anything yet. Maybe his adrenaline went into overdrive after he was hit? You know, fight or flight concept? I've seen it happen after seeing someone shot. So don't make assumptions. You can hypothesize until the cows come home, Trixie, but we have no conclusions to draw from."

I heard the warning in his tone. In other words,

slow my roll. But note to self, ask Solomon about the make and model of this steed of steel, or at least the color, the location of this alleged event, and whether he saw anyone else around.

"So none of that group saw anything at all?"

Higgs clucked his tongue. "Well, here's the word on *that*. Apparently, Agnar bet that guy Edwin—"

"The man who thinks I'm a good person." Coop crowed while I fought a giggle when Higgs gave me a questioning look.

Later, I mouthed.

"Anyway, Agnar bet Edwin he could beat him to the finish line. He was almost a mile ahead of the rest of the pack. So if he really was hit, there's a chance no one saw it—not from his group, anyway. But maybe someone on the sidewalk or a shop owner saw something. The guys at the Cobbler Cove precinct will do a sweep and canvass the area, I'm sure. If it comes to that, I mean. If it was a heart attack, then game over."

Another note to self: Find out bike route and talk to shop owners, but only if this becomes a criminal investigation. Otherwise, you have a shop to run, Trixie Lavender. Mind your p's and q's and run your shop.

"So they're all still at the station now? Did anyone bring them clothes, see if they need something to eat? I can tell you from experience, the hospitality there gets a solid two stars from me on Yelp. And that's only because someone was kind enough to give me directions to the bathroom. Otherwise, it's a bust."

Higgs laughed as Knuckles's phone buzzed, and when he pulled it from the pocket of his leather vest, we all sat up in rapt attention. He'd been waiting to hear from Myer Blackmoore, his client and longtime acquaintance, but I'd begun to think we wouldn't hear anything until morning.

From the look on Knuckles's face—a sour one, by the way—whatever the message was, it couldn't be good.

"Knuck? You okay?" I asked, my concern for him real after what Goose said.

"It's Suzanne. She's afraid to go back to her hotel room alone, but the police have released her—for now, anyway."

Goose cleared his throat but stuck to his original promise to keep his lips zipped. Yet, I knew from the look on his aging face, he was dying to give his input.

I gave Knuckles a sympathetic smile. "Afraid to go to her hotel room? Why?"

He shrugged his wide shoulders and scooted forward on the couch. "Her husband's dead and everyone else is still being questioned. Maybe she just doesn't want to be alone. Would you want to be alone right after your husband died?"

Okay, point. I'm not sure what it'd be like to have a husband, but my heart ached for her anyway. "What can we do for her? How can we help?"

He rose, his solid frame looming over me. "I'm gonna go pick her up and bring her back to my house. She can stay there until the police say she can leave town or whatever it is they do after they're done investigating."

Lifting my hips, I reached in my pocket for my keys. "You can't bring her home on the bike, Knuckles. Take the Caddy and go get her. We'll go back to the house and make something for her to eat."

"How will you get home if I have your car, Trixie girl? I'm pretty sure Mr. Cranky Pants won't like the back of the bike," he said, making Livingston ruffle his feathers.

"I got them, Knuckles. You go get Suzanne. You can ride in with Trix and Coop tomorrow. I'll keep an eye on the bike tonight. Just move it 'round back at the shelter. No worries, friend," Higgs offered with a smile.

Knuckles slapped him on the back and shook his hand, but he wasn't smiling, his face was as somber as I've ever seen it. "Thanks, buddy. See you in a little while." He took off out the door without a backward glance, leaving us all to ponder Suzanne.

Goose was the first to speak as he rose and picked up his coffee mug and shook his head. "You mark my words, that woman is poison and she always will be. He's still runnin' after her just like he used to, cleanin' up her messes. I'm not sayin' another word about it because it stirs up Knuck, but she's no good, Trixie. Never has been, never will be, and I don't care how pretty she still is. She's bad news, and I don't want nothin' to do with it."

I reached a hand out and patted his arm to soothe his ruffled feathers. "You're a good friend, Goose. He's just caught up in the moment of seeing her. You know how it is, right? Sometimes you forget all about the bad and can only focus on the good times when you see someone after years apart. Once he sees more clearly, I'm sure he'll understand why you stated your concerns and all will be well."

Tipping his coffee mug at me, I noted his deep-set hazel eyes flash all manner of emotions. But I guess he decided it wasn't worth creating more trouble. "I'm too close to the situation because of that dang woman's history. You keep an eye on him. That's all I'm askin'."

"Will do," I reassured him with a smile, hoping to alleviate his fears.

With that, he took his cup to the small kitchenette we had in the back of the store without another word, leaving us all to ponder Suzanne.

Well, all of us except for Coop. She already knew Suzanne was bad news.

When she looked over at me, her gaze steady as a rock, she lifted an eyebrow. "I told you she had a bad aura."

❧

"Here you go, Suzanne." I handed her a steaming cup of some crazy mixture of herbs and tea leaves she'd insisted was the only thing she drank at night aside from water. It was what kept her looking so youthful, according to her.

I rather felt like that youthful glow had more to do

with Botox, but what do I know. The only skincare I use is soap and water and a clean towel. My priorities had little to do with anything other than having my hair brushed and clean. I didn't know how to use makeup or curl my hair—among the many things nuns don't do very often.

Coop, who sat as far away from Suzanne as possible with one eye on the television playing in the living room, eyeballed her from across the room as though this aura of hers were rising in toxic steam from the top of her head.

When Suzanne wasn't looking, I squinted to see if I could see what Coop saw, but I didn't see anything except for the glorious, curly mane of hers, so coppery red and shiny, I bet it hurt to look at in the sunlight.

"Is there anything else I can get you, Suzanne?" I asked as we sat around Knuckles's beautiful kitchen island, hoping to ease her fears while we waited for more news on Agnar's death.

She'd acquired clothes from somewhere, a slim-fitting pair of skinny jeans that enhanced her curves and a flowing Bohemian top in yellow with small blue flowers that clung to her figure in all the right places.

While we'd waited for Knuckles to arrive with her, I'd done some research on Suzanne Rothschild-Andrews-Stigsson. Yep, that's her full name, hyphens and all. She's had a couple of husbands since she and Knuckles broke up. A couple of very *rich* husbands.

If you looked at her Facebook page, she was as good as Hollywood royalty. There were tons of pictures of her with famous people, at lavish parties, one where she was even on a yacht. Yet, if you believed what IMDB said, she'd done a lot of movies that didn't even classify as D-listers, and her score from Rotten Tomatoes was pretty rough.

Though, I found it very interesting the bulk of her work was in horror movies—she was a scream queen, and certainly that accounted for her dramatic flair.

In fact, she had a semi-decent following on her Facebook and Instagram pages—if you read the comments, they were mostly from men, young and old, some who'd followed her around since her career began. That she was an actress made perfect sense. She certainly had the pretty pout and the exaggerated facial expressions down pat.

When she looked up at me, she paused for what felt like forever as she scrutinized my face and my clothes —which I'm sure in her world were about as far from designer as one could get. I mean, I'd gotten my overalls at a used clothing store, for golly's sake, not some pop-up exclusive boutique in LA. I guess I couldn't blame her when her style was so effortless.

"Suzanne?" I repeated. "Is there anything else you'd like?"

"No, thank you, Tipsy. I'm fine with this." She held up the mug and gave me a small smile.

"It's *Trixie*," Coop said from the other end of the glossy island. "*Sister* Trixie Lavender."

My eyebrow shot up as I glanced in Coop's direction. Was I hearing a snippy response from my normally unmoved demon? Whatever was the world coming to?

Suzanne eyeballed Coop, sucking in her cheeks. "My apologies, *Sister Trixie*," she cooed in her sultry voice, her eyes never leaving Coop's face.

It was then I recognized what was happening right under my nose. Suzanne had virtually ignored Coop since she'd sashayed into Knuckles's house like royalty. I thought it was due to the fact that Coop came off very aloof, even standoffish, and that could be interpreted as self-involved and maybe even conceited, considering her incredible beauty. But that wasn't it at all.

Suzanne had a case of the green-eyed monsters. Coop was a stunning woman—near flawless—and if I've said it once, I've said it a thousand times, that's no exaggeration and said with zero malice.

Sometimes, you just had to call a spade a spade. Suzanne was certainly beautiful, but she was fading fast, and so far I hadn't seen anyone who could hold a candle to Coop. For someone who was likely used to adoration all day long, who relied on their looks the way Suzanne did, it had to be hard to run into someone like Coop.

I got the distinct impression Suzanne was feeling her age, and Coop didn't make her feel any better, with her lithe body and youthful glow. Then I felt like a dreadful person for thinking those thoughts.

In order to be a good person, you couldn't go around judging a book by its cover, and I was going to stop doing so this second. Her husband was dead.

Maybe these wild swings of emotion had to do with that, and weren't a proper representation of who Suzanne really is.

"I'm just Trixie now. I'm an ex-nun," I said, smiling at her as I fought wrinkling my nose over the stench of her tea. Whatever the concoction was, Knuckles had woken Liam from Ye Old Spice Shop, a place to buy exotic tea and spices, in order to please Suzanne. Or was that appease? I wasn't sure.

"How interesting," she drawled before she sighed, long and wistful.

"Suzanne? Meet Noodles and Biscuit," Knuckles said proudly as he carried his two cats out into the kitchen and held them up for her to see.

Livingston, who perched on the bar Knuckles had specifically hung in the kitchen for him, so he'd always be with us on movie nights and during meals, stirred.

While Jeff was learning to be a dog, Livingston was fighting his urge to be an owl, and Noodles and Biscuit were prime prey.

Suzanne held her hands out to the felines, gathering Noodles, a gorgeous calico, in her arms when Knuckles handed her over. But Noodles squirmed out of her grasp, fighting to get away and scratching her on her bare arm. She took off back into Knuckles's bedroom, the pads of her paws skidding on the hardwood floor, with Biscuit hot on her heels.

Suzanne hissed a bad word and, almost as if on cue, her eyes welled with fat teardrops. She held up her arm and showed Knuckles the small scratch, her bottom lip quivering. "I'm going to scar, Donald! I have a movie in less than three weeks and I'm the slowest healer ever. Hurry! Do you have some antibiotic cream?"

Cheese and rice already. I'd been shot in the foot and I didn't cry—not even a tear, and believe you me, it more than stung. I was starting to think, even though I wanted to give her a real chance, Goose was right.

Coop jumped up from her stool and called out, "I'll get it." Meanwhile, Knuckles went about soothing her.

Instantly, his face was crestfallen. "Jeez, Suz. I'm sorry. Noodles is usually pretty easygoing around strangers. Maybe she's just having a bad day. Does it hurt?"

Suzanne pouted. "Like the dickens."

Coop returned with the antibiotic cream, and I watched as Suzanne all but ignored my demon and held her arm up to Knuckles and whispered, "Would you, please, Donald?"

Just then, Higgs pushed the front door open, carrying no less than five—*five*—suitcases. Pretty fancy ones, too, if you ask me. I rushed over to help him, grabbing the handle of one pink suitcase that felt like she'd packed it with lead.

"What the heck is in these?" Higgs whispered to me under his breath as he huffed his way in the door.

He'd offered to handle Suzanne's luggage while Knuckles got her settled, but I bet he was regretting that offer now.

"Probably whatever she takes to stay looking so young, and at fifty that's probably calls for a lot of product," I replied, then immediately regretted my words. "Sorry. That was rude and uncalled for. I don't know where my reaction to her is coming from."

Higgs snickered as he hauled the cluster of suitcases into the middle of the living room. "It's nice to see the human side of you, Trixie, even if it has a meow tacked on the end of the sentence. I think she rubs you the wrong way because of what Goose said, and you want to protect Knuckles because he's your friend. It's very human."

I didn't say anything while I pondered how petty I was being as I looked down at her multitude of bags.

"I thought Knuckles said they were only going to be here for three days. Who packs this much for *three days* —especially when part of the time they're going to be naked?"

I giggled. "Suzanne does, dahling," I drawled.

As we managed to corral all her luggage, we both stopped when we saw the local late-night news on Knuckles's flat-screen TV. Higgs reached for the remote to turn up the sound.

"In local news," the pretty reporter with blonde hair and a toothy smile said, "an LA man was killed today during the World Naked Bike Ride in the Cobbler Cove District of Portland. Sources tell Action News Ten, the police are calling this a homicide, but won't comment further. A thorough investigation is under-way. For the latest, join us tomorrow morning…"

Everything faded away but the sound of Suzanne's shriek. I can tell you true, she wasn't a scream queen for nothing. I'm sure my ears will ring for days to come.

Then she fainted. Just crumbled right in the middle of Knuckles's hardwood floor as though she were melting ice cream under the hot July sun, her hair fanning out behind her, arm sprawled across her forehead.

And still, even in a dead faint, even with help from whatever she used to stay so youthful, I couldn't believe she was fifty.

Do wonders never cease?

CHAPTER 7

"Suzanne!" Knuckles patted her dewy-soft cheek as she lay on his ultra-comfy couch, his face riddled with worry.

The second she'd dropped almost gracefully, if that were at all possible, was the second Knuckles scooped her up off the floor and carried her to the couch as though she were a mere feather.

"Suzanne! Wake up!" he repeated, pressing the cool cloth I'd run and grabbed against her forehead.

Her eyes fluttered open slowly, her long eyelashes fanning against her high cheekbones. "Donald?" she whispered. "Tell me it's not real. Tell me the police don't think someone killed Agnar! Who would do such a thing, Donald? It can't be real!"

"But it is real," Coop stated in her matter-of-fact way. "That's exactly what they said. See?" She grabbed Higgs's phone from him and held it under Suzanne's nose to show her the text Tansy had just sent.

"Coop!" I reprimanded on a soft hiss of words, nudging her in the ribs. "Give that back to Higgs."

But my demon was undaunted by my admonishment. "I was only telling the truth. You told me to always tell the truth, and that's the truth. They think Agnar was killed. That's what the word *homicide* means."

Higgs put his hand on Coop's shoulder, taking over for me, because I think he sensed I wanted to strangle her. I know she's still learning all the subtleties of being human, and I know as a onetime nun, I should be more patient (which, by the by, is probably why I was considering leaving the convent anyway), but I'd had a long day and I was a little frazzled.

He held out his other hand and waited for Coop to place the phone in his palm, which she did, but not without the death glare. "Coop, Suzanne's distressed. Let's be sensitive to that, yes? I know you're only trying to help, and your honesty is always appreciated, but time and place, if you get my meaning."

Coop—my emotionless demon—rolled her eyes at Higgs. *Rolled. Her. Eyes.* To say I was shocked is to say a category five hurricane is just a passing storm.

In her best impression of Alexis Carrington from *Dynasty*, she lifted her chin and flipped her hair over her shoulder and huffed (yes! huffed). "Then if you'll excuse me, I'm going to go feed Livingston." With that, she sauntered off to the kitchen without looking back, her shoulders squared, her head held high.

Both Higgs and I looked at one another as we

fought a snicker. Coop loved old reruns of *Dynasty*, and for some reason, she'd decided to model herself after the characters.

I'm guessing it was because she thought they displayed all of the emotions she so desired. What she didn't understand was how extra they were—how they emoted everything to the nth degree.

"We'd better pay closer attention to what our Coop's watching, Miss Lavender. We can't have her copying JR Ewing. I don't know if you remember, but he did get shot," Higgs whispered on a snort.

Which made me really have to fight to keep from laughing out loud. Instead, I yanked his arm to pull him closer and gave him a stern look. "Knock it off, Higglesworth. We have a serious situation here. Straighten up and fly right, buddy, before Knuckles boots us out on our behinds."

"Don't you mean butt-ox?" he asked, and that was all I could take. I literally had to stuff my fingers in my mouth and cross my legs to keep from giggling like a loon or worse, wetting myself.

"Donald," Suzanne said, sitting up and sweeping away the cloth on her forehead. "You have to help me! I have to know who killed Agnar! We can't let whomever it is get away with it! How will I go on without answers? They'll blame *me*, Donald. They always blame the wife! Please say you'll help me, Donnie!"

Knuckles sat back on his couch and frowned. "Isn't that what the police are for?"

She planted a hand on his arm and squeezed , her

coral-painted nails sinking into his lightly tanned flesh. "Didn't you just tell me on the way over here that you and Tipsy solved a murder last month?"

"*It's Trixie*," Coop said with a raised voice from the kitchen.

In fact, it almost sounded as though we could put an exclamation point on the end of her sentence, it was so emphatic. What the heck was happening to my demon?

But Suzanne merely waved her delicate hand in the air, her eyes beseeching. "Trixie, Dixie, Mitzie, whatever. Her name's not the point. Isn't that what you told me, Donnie? That you people solved a murder."

I have to tell you, it was stranger than strange the way she called Knuckles Donnie or even Donald. I know that's his given name, but it was almost like a pet name she'd used back in a time when they'd shared intimacies I neither wanted to know nor hear about.

I can't say why, but it made me uncomfortable, and not only because they'd been intimate and Knuckles was a lot like a father figure to me. It made me uncomfortable for reasons I can't put my finger on.

"No," Knuckles corrected. "I didn't say we solved the murder. I was telling you what's been happening in my life since I last saw you, and what led me to Cobbler Cove. Then I said I tried to help *Trixie* solve a murder so she could get back into Inkerbelle's and we could open the shop. We all tried to help because Higgs's neck was on the line."

I held up a finger, moving closer to them, my gaze meeting Suzanne's. "What Knuckles says is true. I sort of just *happened* upon the murderer. It wasn't my expert sleuthing skills that found the killer."

Suzanne sat up on her haunches, tucking her feet under her, her ultra-blue eyes on fire. "But isn't the nice-looking one a police officer? I seem to remember you babbling about someone involved in law enforcement, right, Donald?"

Higgs sucked in his cheeks, and as I grew more confident at reading his emotions, I could tell he was annoyed. But if I wasn't sure, I can tell you this—it seeped into his tone of voice enough that I heard his irritation.

He looked Suzanne directly in the eye and took on an authoritative stance. "It's Higgs or *Cross Higglesworth*, Mrs. Stigsson, and yes, I was an under-cover police officer. But I'm retired, and now I own the Peach Street men's shelter, which takes up a great deal of my time. I don't do police work anymore."

She threw her shoulders back and thrust her chest forward, her eyes filling with tears as she reached out a hand and placed it on Higgs's biceps, giving him a gentle squeeze.

"Oh, call me Suzanne, and won't you consider helping me, Cross? *Please?*" she whispered in a watery voice as a single tear trickled down her creamy cheek. "You obviously have connections, resources, and you know your way around a crime scene. Certainly you know they always blame the wife? Please help me. I wouldn't even know where to begin…"

Wowwowwow, was she ever good at the "you're the

big strong man and I'm the helpless female" act. She didn't say as much in words, it had more to do with the lilt of her demure tone, the strategically placed hand on Higgs's arm, the flutter of her eyelashes.

And I promise you, if he fell for this cutesy, flirty nonsense, I was going to knock him into next Tuesday. But he remained unmoved, or at least he appeared as such. Probably due to the fact that he was used to all sorts of people, sultry women included, trying to bribe him into doing things.

Higgs stuck his hands in the pockets of his jeans and rocked back on his sneakered feet. "Like Knuckles…er *Donnie* said, I'm not sure why you wouldn't just let the police handle this, Mrs. Stigsson. That's what we pay taxes for."

But Suzanne wasn't going to let Higgs off the hook. If anything, she ramped up the charm by calling up more tears. "I can't have this marring my good name! I'm due on a movie set in Canada in three weeks. If this drags on, and they won't let me leave, how will I ever pay the bills?"

With all the money your rich husbands pay you in alimony?

Boy, I really had the devil in me tonight, didn't I? No pun intended. I shook off my inner thoughts. I didn't know if that was true. Maybe she didn't get alimony from anyone, but surely Agnar had plenty of money? He did hang around with a world-renowned chef who owned a bunch of restaurants all over the world. Didn't money attract money?

"Suzanne," Knuckles intercepted by patting her hand. "How about we talk this over in the morning. It's late, and you need some sleep."

Suddenly, her entire body deflated. Her shoulders sagged and her eyes shot to the floor. "You're right. I'm utterly exhausted. It's been the most horrid day, Donnie. So horrid."

Knuckles bounced his head up and down. "Then let me help you to your room. You can get comfortable and get some rest, okay?" He grabbed her hand and pulled her up from the couch, but before she allowed him to lead her off to the back bedrooms, her small frame resting against his, she said, "Please think about it, Tipsy. *Please!*"

Both Higgs and I took deep breaths as we looked at one another in wonder.

He was the first to speak as he leaned into me. "*Wow.*"

"Tell me about it. You know she's an actress, right? A scream queen, according to IMDB and her Facebook page."

"You know, I would have pegged her for a mild-mannered librarian. Color me all sorts of shocked."

My index finger immediately went to my mouth. "Shhh. She'll hear us."

Higgs made a face. "Can she hear anything but the sound of her own voice?"

"She's right," Coop called out. "If I can hear you, so can she."

. . .

J fought a snicker. "Maybe not, but Knuckles might. Honest, Higgs, I don't want him involved in anything that could lead to him being hurt."

"You think he still has a thing for her?"

I sighed, mostly because I didn't know for sure. "I don't know. You know how old feelings can be when you're feeling vulnerable."

Higgs gave me a look of concern. "Is he feeling vulnerable? What's going on?"

Sighing, I bit the inside of my cheek before answering. "He's been a little sad lately. I think he's missing Candice and sometimes just when you think the death of a loved one is getting easier to deal with, you get punched in the gut. Anyway, I know for sure he seems oblivious to Suzanne's phony act. He's giving her a pass based on the theory people change. You know how that can be. With time comes perspective, and with perspective comes the maturity of realizing the mistakes you made and making excuses for the mistakes others have made, too. We glorify—or maybe a better word is memorialize—relationships from the past and forget about the harm they caused our hearts."

"How would you know about romantic relationships, Sister Trixie?" he asked with a teasing smile.

"It may not have been romantic, but I was in the biggest relationship of all, remember? You know, with the man upstairs? Hence, I know what it's like to make excuses for missteps or things that don't make sense.

You forget them or sweep them under the rug in favor of the bigger picture."

Higgs eyed me thoughtfully. "Have I ever told you how sage you are for someone so young? You make me rethink everything I thought I believed in."

I grinned at him, crossing my arms over my chest. "That can't be good. I can't have you doubting your relationship with a good cheeseburger. What is Higgs without beef?"

He barked a laugh, the grooves on either side of his face deepening. "I do love a good cheeseburger. My bovine love aside, what can we do to help Knuckles?"

Wrinkling my nose, I looked at the wall in Knuckles's dining room, full of beautifully framed pictures, and sighed. "You're not going to like what I have to say."

"On the contrary. I almost always like what you have to say. Unless you say you have leftovers of that crazy chicken meatball noodle soup you make. I don't like when you say that because it means I'm going to get a Tupperware bowl full of the stuff."

Reaching over, I pinched his arm and made a face. "Stop teasing me about that soup. It's not that bad. Anyway, here's what I'm going to say. You do realize she's going to pressure Knuckles into talking us into helping her, and he will, because he still hasn't had a recent enough reminder of what she was like back in the day—if she really was a viper like Goose says. Maybe I'm just reading her wrong, and she has changed, but you have to admit, she's pretty dramatic about pretty much *everything*."

His dark eyes narrowed, the soft lighting from the living room lamps illuminating them. "Are you saying *we* should help her?"

"I'm saying we should help *Knuckles*. He's all I care about, Higgs. I'm sorry Suzanne's husband is dead, but I'm not a fan of her big doe eyes and her hair twirl. Everything she does is so…I dunno. Over the top is the expression, maybe? Had you ever even heard of her before tonight? Because I sure hadn't. But then, I was a nun for a long time. We didn't frequent the Cineplex for sinners on the reg."

Higgs laughed. "I'm not much of a horror fan. I'm more *Fast and Furious* than I am *Texas Chainsaw Massacre*. So, no. I didn't recognize her, but she sure behaves like I should have known who she is."

"Regardless, will you help me help him?"

Higgs eyed me, his smile facetious. "Aside from helping Knuckles, this wouldn't have anything to do with your love of a good murder mystery, would it, Sister Trixie? And don't fib, because it's not nice for ex-nuns to tell tales out of school. Besides, I'll know. I am an ex-undercover police officer, you know," he said on a wink.

I thought about that for a moment. I didn't want to appear like some ambulance chaser, but I did want Suzanne out of the picture. I know, I know. As an ex-nun, you're probably thinking rather than scorn her, I should try and talk to her about the way she approaches getting what she wants with all that cooing, cutesy nonsense. The way I would anyone else who behaved the way she does.

But she rankled me, and I'm honest enough to admit it's because Knuckles is so dear to me—to us. And fine, in the interest of honesty, I love a good murder mystery and any excuse to snoop is good enough for me, okay? There. I said it. I felt a tingle I can't quite describe when the news anchor said Agnar's death was a homicide.

I don't wish ill on anyone ever. But bad things happen all the time, so there might as well be someone like me who was willing to get in the trenches and find out who did the bad thing, right? It's sort of similar to service to my community, right?

Looking Higgs in the eyes, I chose my words carefully. "I will neither confirm nor deny my interest in solving a murder, but I will tell you, I can't do it without some help. I trust you, Higgs. You know the ropes. You know people who know the ropes, and while I'd never ask you to use your contacts to my advantage, I'd at least like to ask you for your advice."

"Then consider it a done deal, Mitzie," he teased.

"That's Tipsy to you, buster."

We both laughed then covered our mouths so as not to disturb the sleeping superstar.

And then I got serious.

Standing on tiptoe, I pressed a quick kiss to Higgs's cheek, the scent of his fresh cologne I'd grown to love staying in my nostrils long after I pulled away.

I'm not normally so forward (heck, I'm not *ever* forward), but sometimes impulse gets the better of me. Not to mention, I was grateful to him for agreeing to help without dragging me through the mud and taunting me about the drool forming at the corner of my mouth.

"Thanks, Higgs. I really appreciate this."

When his hand went to my waist, we both paused a moment, our breathing uneven, before we pulled away.

I didn't have time to reflect on the funny jumble my insides were experiencing. I had work to do. But maybe afterward, when we'd hopefully figured this out, I'd delve deeper into my reaction to him.

Higgs winked at me. "You bet, Sister Trixie. Anything for you."

I winced. "I bet you won't be saying that when I'm driving you nuts with my theories."

"We'll see. But we have to have rules, Trixie. Rules you follow no matter what. Deal?"

Right now, I didn't care what the rules were. I only cared that Knuckles didn't end up hurt and Suzanne went back to Hollywood.

So I agreed, sticking out my hand. "Deal."

He shook my hand and grinned. "Okay. I have to get back to the shelter. I'm sure Jeff's chewing something up. Not to mention my favorite troublemaker, Mario, has turned up again, and you know how territorial he can get over that bed by the window. The staff says he's giving Griffin a hard time about it."

I loved Griffin. He was sweet and soft-spoken and

terrified of the dark. He was always the first in line to get a bed for the night at the Guy-MCA. "You tell Griff I said hello. He likes my chicken meatball soup, by the way."

Higgs made a face at me. "No. That's not true. He lies and says he likes it because he doesn't want to hurt your feelings due to the fact that he thinks you're pretty. I think Griffin has a little crush on you, Miss Lavender."

I gave him a playful poke in his chest. "Is that how you know someone has a crush on you? When they eat your soup even though they think it's yucky?"

"That's a sure sign. At least one sure sign."

"You make no bones about telling me you hate my soup. I guess I know where I stand with you then, don't I?" I teased, before I realized what I'd said could come off as flirtatious.

He headed toward Knuckles's front door, hands in his pockets, but his eyes gleamed. "I don't know that you do, Sister Trixie. I don't know that you do."

My cheeks went flaming hot, the way they always do when I'm embarrassed.

Lately, they'd been flaming hot around Higgs more than I cared to admit.

And that was curious.

Curious, indeed.

CHAPTER 8

*B*right and early the next day, I was more than ready to play amateur detective. I banged on Higgs's dark green apartment door at seven a.m. sharp. He lived in a swanky high-rise overlooking the Willamette, not far from the shelter, with lots of glass and steel, totally the opposite from Knuckles's house, which was warm and homey. But it was still very appealing, with all its sleek lines and fun metal art sculptures in the lobby.

He told me he'd bought the apartment after he'd retired from the force because he loved the amazing view of the mountains and the river, and while it was very manly, with a lot of hardwood ceilings and iron-work, I had to admit, the view really was amazing.

I'd had a restless night, spent worried about Knuckles and his ex-girlfriend. I got up before the sun and watched the news, hoping for more information, but the report mirrored the one from the night before with no new details.

Naturally, because I don't know how to stop myself since I'd discovered this urge to solve mysteries, I hypothesized well into the wee hours of the morning, tossing and turning in my big king-size bed with so many throw pillows, my head would never lack support.

Many of my theories revolved around Suzanne being a serial killer who'd killed all of her prior husbands by some nefarious means. Which meant I was being woefully petty, and I regretted that. But we couldn't ignore the fact that she'd been through a few marriages.

Now, showered and dressed, my morning devotions done (it's not exactly the traditional devotion. I simply map out goals for myself for the day and spend some quiet time listening to the silence), coffee in hand and one for Higgs from Betty's, the itch to get a move on was real.

"Trixie?" a very sleepy Higgs said from beyond the crack in his apartment door.

"Reporting for duty," I joked, giving him a salute and a smile.

He squinted at me. "Do you know what time it is?"

"Time for us to catch a killer."

"Oooor," he drawled on a yawn, scratching the part of his chest exposed in his bathrobe. "Time for overzealous ex-nuns to go away and come back at a more reasonable hour. I was at the shelter until four this morning, sorting out Mario and Griffin. Cal's covering for me this morning."

Cal Hallows being the social worker he'd hired who'd grown tired of the system, and the limitations it placed on him, and had decided to deal with the community in need directly. I liked Cal a lot. He was a thirty-something nerd who loved all things *Star Wars* and football.

I held up the cup of coffee and shook it at him. "But I brought coffee, strong and black. Just the way you like it—with a hint of hickory. That should help get your engine started."

He popped the door open wide to reveal the rest of his blue-and-white striped bathrobe cinched at his waist. I was grateful Jeff bounded toward the door at me, jumping up on my thighs and almost knocking me over, distracting me from Higgs and his nightwear.

I'm still a little unsure what's appropriate and what isn't in male-female relationships. I never dated much before I entered the convent because I was too wrapped up doing drugs. Not that Higgs and I are dating, mind you. That's not what I mean at all.

I just don't know male-female protocols for a friendship, what's acceptable and what isn't. I didn't know if I should look away, so I kept my eyes on Jeff.

"Jeff! No! That's not nice. Down, Jeff, down!" Higgs reprimanded, grabbing him by the collar to pull him off me.

I winked down at Jeff. He really is the cutest, even

when he's knocking me around, trying to be the best dog he knows how to be.

"Hey, little man. You ready to help catch a killer?" Jeff let out a bark I found myself pretty impressed with. He was dogging like a champ these days. All that YouTube was paying off. "See? Jeff's ready."

Higgs ran a hand through his thick hair, which, by the way, didn't look like he'd been sleeping at all, leaving me feeling a little jealous. "Jeff needs to potty, and seeing as you're disturbing my beauty sleep and I haven't even showered yet, I'll take that coffee, thank you very much, and grab a shower. You can take Jeff out for potties, Detective Lavender." He reached down and scratched Jeff's head with a fond smile. "You gotta go potties, bud?"

Jeff ran around in circles, another sure sign he was paying attention to the videos he'd been watching.

I stepped inside and held out my hand for the leash. "Fifteen minutes, partner. That's all you get. I have to be at the shop at noon. I want to cover as much ground as possible this morning before I have to open. I have a list of things we should do and people we should talk to. I've already looked up Agnar and his friends on social media, so I'm more familiar with our suspects. Want me to run what I found out by you?"

"Pushy, pushy," he said on a groan, taking a long gulp of his coffee. "Save your list for after my coffee, Sleuth. I'm barely functioning."

Peering up at him, I nodded my understanding, but that didn't stop me from telling him what I'd found on

Agnar. "So you don't want to know that he's a rich art dealer, dealing in exotic and rare pieces?"

"I want to know everything you've gathered, my little Nancy Drew, *after* my coffee."

I rolled my eyes, adjusting the strap of my purse over my shoulder. "Fine. Coffee before murder, but before I take our boy here for a walk, any more news from Tansy you can share?"

He shook his head, his eyes direct if not still full of sleep. "Not a word. As far as I know, nothing's changed. They're calling it homicide, but I have no idea why because I didn't see any signs of foul play."

I nodded, staring out the floor-to-ceiling windows splayed across his entire living room just beyond his brown leather couch. "Me neither, but they know something we don't, for sure."

"They're probably waiting on the coroner's report for anything definitive. We might want to do that, too, before we jump through hoops."

"Oh, no, Mr. Play-It-Safe. We don't have time to wait. Do you know what that woman did last night after you left?"

He gave me a skeptical glance over his coffee cup. "I don't know, but I'm pretty sure you're going to tell me…"

"She asked Knuckles to go outside and cover the solar landscaping lights because the shades in her bedroom weren't enough to block out the glare. It was too much for her delicate sensibilities." I said, mimicking her words from the night before.

Higgs tipped his cup at me. "Wow. Nice Suzanne impression. You're pretty good at that breathy, sultry thing she does with her voice."

I ignored his praise in favor of my anger. "Do you know how many landscaping lights Knuckles has, Higgs?"

He winced, shoving a hand into the pocket of his bathrobe. "A lot?"

I pointed my finger in the air. "That's right. A. Lot. Oooh, that woman infuriates me, Higgs!"

"Did he really do it?"

I snorted in disdain. "With bells on, he did, tripping all over himself the entire way while she took a long hot bath. She's the worst, and she's taking advantage of him. I think Goose was spot on about her. I don't think her mistakes had anything to do with youth. I think she's just mean. Now, get that shower, because the sooner she goes back to wherever she came from, the sooner we can all go back to normal."

"I'm on it," he said, turning his back to us to head for his very white, very marble bathroom.

I latched Jeff's leash to his collar and gave him a tug toward the door, closing it behind me. "C'mon, buddy. I need to walk off some of this steam or it's going to come out of my ears."

"She's a wicked piece a work, huh, Trixie?" Jeff asked from below.

I hit the elevator button and huffed an aggravated breath. "If you only knew. Knuckles is at the market right now because concentrated orange juice is processed and Suzanne can't put processed food in her temple of a body. She only drinks fresh. The poor man was up half the night covering landscaping lights, and then back up at the crack of dawn to go get what she needs for breakfast."

Jeff scampered next to me as we got on the elevator, his claws clacking on the tile. "This isn't like you, Trixie. You never complain about anything. She's really got ya all twisted up."

I narrowed my eyes. Just the thought of Suzanne rankled, and I couldn't seem to stop it from showing. "She's horrible, Jeff. I hate the way she's abusing Knuckles and his penchant for protecting and nurturing the people he cares about."

"Ya think he's still got a thing for her?"

My stomach sank at the thought as I watched the display of floor numbers drop until we stopped at the lobby. "I think he's just in a bad place in his life, missing Candice like he has lately, but I hope not. I *really* hope not. And she'd better not have a thing for *him*. She's been a widow for two-point-two whole seconds. She should be grieving, not toying with a man she did wrong and hasn't seen in decades."

The elevator door popped open with a ding, and I stalked out of it, all worked up. As we made our way to the revolving glass door, I inhaled a cleansing breath, trying to rid myself of my ill will toward Suzanne. Everyone had an off day. Maybe Suzanne was having one last night and I was unfairly reacting to her demands. Today was a new day and I was going to start it with a clean slate.

The weather had finally turned a bit cooler after an almost month-long heat wave, and I was determined to enjoy the breeze from the river as we took off down the sidewalk to Jeff's favorite potty spot. The sun shined in all its glory, an orange ball of happiness, making me smile.

People hustled along the sidewalk in their colorful Portland array. One of the things I loved most about Portland was the diversity here. I loved that everything was so casual, me being a jeans-and-T-shirt kind of girl, or you could dress up and no one batted an eye.

Without warning, a man dressed in a casual plaid button-down shirt, blue jeans and brown loafers jumped out from between the two buildings we were just about to pass. "Trixie Lavender?"

My eyes opened in surprise as I stopped when he blocked my path, his eager gaze glued to mine. "Who are you?"

He stuck out a wide hand, his cheerfully youthful smile the exact opposite of his blue eyes, which were icy and hard. "Ben Adams. I'm a journalist for *Truth Seeker Confidential* magazine."

I'd never heard of his magazine, but then, I haven't really joined the rest of the planet on what's current. I'm still working on getting the gist of social media, for Pete's sake. So was it a reputable magazine or a tabloid? Still, I was hesitant to engage. Why would someone from a magazine want to talk to me?

But I stuck out my hand anyway and let him envelop mine, giving his a firm shake. "Do I know you? Or maybe the better question is, how do you know me?"

"Can you tell me how you know Suzanne Rothschild?" He used the name she worked professionally under, making me pause before I remembered she didn't use Stigsson.

"Can you tell me how you think you *know* that I know Suzanne Rothschild?" I asked, dumbfounded by his question.

He smiled pleasantly. Yet, I couldn't help but get the impression he was pleased with himself. "It's my job to know. It's called research. So can you tell me what her state of mind is today?"

I frowned and tried to step around him, tugging Jeff's leash to lead him away, but Ben hopped in front of me, his face still cheerful and bright.

"Miss Lavender? Can you tell me how Suzanne's feeling today after what happened last night? She *is* staying with you at your house, isn't she?"

A chill raced along my spine. How did he know Suzanne was at the house? Had he been following her—us?

That was my cue to shut my mouth. No way was I giving anyone any information about anything. Without giving any thought to much but getting away from him, I said, "I'm sorry, Mr. Adams, but I've never heard of you or your magazine and I don't know what you're talking about. So if you'll excuse me, I need to be on my way."

I tried to step around him while Jeff snarled, barring his teeth, but that only appeared to make him more persistent. He didn't exactly prevent me from getting away from him, but he definitely wasn't going to make it easy.

"Oh, c'mon, Miss Lavender," he said pleasantly. "Can't you give a guy a little something? I gotta make a living, too. Listen, there's money in this for you if you'll give me an exclusive on Suzanne."

My ire began to stir, and I don't mind telling you, I fret over whether that's a trigger for the evil hiding inside me. Though, I had to ask myself, where the demon inside me was now when it could be used for a specific purpose instead of only creating chaos?

Still, getting away from him now was a priority. No one wanted to see an ex-nun go rabid in downtown Portland, and without Coop here to keep me semi in check, his chance for survival was slim.

"I'm sorry, I can't help you, Mr. Adams. Now, if you'll let me pass, I have somewhere to be."

"Can you tell me about Suzanne and the prenup she signed when she married Agnar Stigsson?"

My ears perked. Prenup? Well, I guess that made sense if Agnar was as rich as the rest of her ex-husbands. Shoot, I wanted to know what he was talking about, but I didn't want to play his game and get caught up in speaking out of turn.

So I attempted to step around him again, and I was successful as I turned and began walking back toward

Higgs's apartment…until he sidled up beside me, still cheery and bright.

"Were you aware Agnar Stigsson saw a divorce attorney just a few days before they flew to Portland for the World Naked Bike Ride? And were you also aware Suzanne could be left with nothing but the clothes on her back if he found out she was unfaithful? Did you know there was trouble in their marriage? The prenup says very clearly if Agnar Stigsson files for divorce, she doesn't get a penny."

I tried to keep my jaw from unhinging, but in all the talk last night, she'd made it sound as though he was the love of her life. She'd never once mentioned she and Agnar were on the rocks.

Though, seriously. Would a murderer tell you their marriage was on the brink of divorce if it meant you stood to lose everything? I mean, how would she go on without her special tealeaves and freshly squeezed orange juice?

In prison I don't think those items can be bartered for with maxi-pads and packets of Slim Jims.

CHAPTER 9

My eyes widened and my heart began to throb in my chest over this new information, but I couldn't let this man see my reaction. He'd know I had no idea about a prenup. However, a prenup where Suzanne got nothing didn't look good for her—not good at all.

Question was, did Knuckles know about this?

It was definitely motive for Suzanne to murder her husband if she wanted to prevent him from filing for divorce so she wouldn't lose everything. Obviously, just from the demands she'd made for special teas and irritating landscaping lights, she was accustomed to living a particular lifestyle. One she might not want to give up.

But there wasn't even a hint of strife between the two if you looked at her Facebook and Instagram. Agnar, unlike his very social media savvy wife, didn't use his Facebook page for more than his work as an arts dealer. His Facebook page had tons of pictures of sculptures and paintings, and one really weird vase that didn't look as though it was meant to hold anything.

But he was rich—he just didn't show it off in the way Suzanne did.

Holy cats. Maybe Suzanne wasn't just a not-so-nice, overly dramatic person. Maybe she was a murderer.

"Miss Lavender? Did you hear my question? Did you know Agnar Stigsson saw a prominent divorce attorney only a few days before they flew to Portland?" Ben Adams repeated, his tone changing ever so slightly from falsely pleasant to mildly annoyed.

Ugh. As much as I wanted to know the details about what he had on Suzanne, I didn't want them this way. It felt dirty, and his persistence had begun to make me cranky.

Stopping dead in my tracks, I looked him square in the eye and narrowed my gaze. "I'm going to say this one last time, Mr. Adams, and if you don't stop harassing me, I'm going to call the police. I have *no comment*. I don't know what you're talking about. Now, please, go away!"

My voice rose enough for people to give me strange glances as they bustled past us, going about their day.

Then Higgs was there, freshly showered, dressed in his usual crisp white T-shirt and jeans. Hands in his pockets, he approached me with a question in his eyes. "Trixie? Everything all right?"

"Why don't you ask Ben Adams from *Something-Something-Confidential*?" I asked, handing him Jeff's leash.

"*Truth Seeker Confidential*," Ben corrected affably, holding out a hand to Higgs—one he flat-out ignored.

"And what can we do for you today, Ben Adams from *Truth Seeker Confidential*?" Higgs asked, his eyes scanning Ben's face as he loomed over him.

His grin went from pleasant to cocky. "I was just asking Miss Lavender here if she knew about her friend Suzanne's marriage being on the rocks? Do you know Suzanne Rothschild?" he asked, though he did back up a step.

"Were you then? And what did Miss Lavender have to say, Ben Adams?" he asked from compressed lips, his jaw tight, the muscles in his biceps flexing, making the tattoos on his forearms sharper in the sunlight.

"I said no comment," I replied, my words stiff and curt. "But Ben didn't want to hear that."

Higgs gave me back Jeff's leash and crossed his arms over his wide chest, widening his stance. "Really? Is that true, Ben? Are you harassing Miss Lavender? Gee, I'd hate to think in this day and age, when a lady says no to whatever it is you're asking, you don't understand it means *no*. You do understand the word no, don't you, Ben? I mean, I could call your boss and ask her if you understand what no means—or would you like *me* to explain what no means?"

I liked seeing Higgs like this—so authoritative, so

imposing. It made me feel safe and protected, and while I like to think I can take care of myself, it was nice to have backup. Especially when the backup was big and intimidating, something I'm most definitely not.

When Ben didn't respond, his eyes wide and definitely wary, Higgs popped his lips as he looked down at him. "You know what I think, Ben Adams? I think you should go on about your business and enjoy this lovely day Portland's having. And always remember, no comment means *no comment*." Holding out his arm to me, he said, "Shall we?"

I looped my arm through his, and he tucked it under his strong biceps, guiding me around Ben Adams and down the street until we were out of the intrusive man's earshot.

Then I couldn't contain myself anymore. "First, thank you for stepping in. I'm not so much a feminist that I can't admit he was flustering me, and I needed help. I've never encountered a journalist looking for a scoop before, but you handled that like a champ."

Higgs smiled down at me, his tanned skin gleaming under the bright sun. "I don't doubt you'd have figured it out, Trixie. But I've dealt with the press before. In my line of work, it happened all the time— especially with celebrities as minor as Suzanne's celebrity is."

"Have you heard of *Truth Seeker Confidential* magazine?"

He scoffed and frowned. "It's a rag mag, and hardly

reputable. You did the right thing by keeping your lips sealed."

Yet, the fact that someone wanted a scoop on Suzanne made me wonder. "Maybe Suzanne's a bigger deal than we thought? If a rag mag's looking for an exclusive on her, that is. I know nothing about horror movies, but maybe in that world she's a big deal?"

"I snooped around a little bit online and found she has quite the cult following from her scream queen days. They're small but they're mighty. She's not quite on par with celebs like Elvira in the genre, but in the horror circles, she's not unknown, either. There are some really strange people out there who speculate about her on the daily at this fan site I found, and it doesn't look like she discourages them."

Go figure. "I fell asleep before I got that far last night. Also, I wanted to stuff a sock in her mouth by then, so I couldn't stomach researching more about her, but I did check out Agnar, and he's super rich. Or at least I think he is. As I said before, he's an art dealer. His Facebook page is full of pictures of places he's been all over the world. So if he's not rich, he's certainly not poor. Myer Blackmoore's a rich restaurateur, but you already know that. Edwin Garvey's also a rich guy, but I don't know exactly what he does…or if he does *anything* other than be rich. Lucinda Ferris is a stylist, and I think she's Suzanne's best friend. There are a bunch of pictures on her Facebook page of the two of them at all sorts of Hollywood events. And lastly, Grady Hanson. He's in finance of some sort. He was the one who made the comment about Suzanne and her drama."

Higgs stopped in front of a charming, small café and pointed inside. "Hold those thoughts, would you? Can we grab a little something to eat while we discuss this? I, unlike you, need more than coffee and a hot tip to get my motor running."

I motioned with my hand for him to take a seat at one of the outdoor tables, colorfully decorated with turquoise tablecloths and pink carnations in small bud vases. "Absolutely, and it's my treat for getting you up so early to help."

"Music to my ears."

The sign read: Please Seat Yourself, so Higgs pulled out a white metal chair and helped me get situated.

A waitress approached and brought us menus and as we perused them, I couldn't stop thinking about how Ben Adams knew my name and the fact that I knew Suzanne.

Leaning forward on my elbows, I said, "How do you think that reporter knows my name? How did he even know Suzanne was at the house?"

Higgs looked up from his menu, an eyebrow cocked. "Because that's what the paps do. They hunt down their victims and make it their business to sink their claws into anyone even remotely close to the person they're about to slander with half-truths. I'm sure he got wind of the fact that Suzanne was here for the ride, because she made no bones about it all over her Facebook page. Then he saw the news or someone tipped him off, and the only thing he had to do was show up at the police station where Suzanne was detained and be creepy enough to follow Knuckles and Suzanne home. It happens all the time."

I shivered, rubbing my arms. Even though the day was warming up, I felt cold. To think someone had been following us unnerved me to no end.

"I hear disdain in your voice for these types of journalists. Bad experience?"

Higgs's face went hard, his rigid jaw tightening. "Many. They were the bane of my existence on the force—mostly had to do with sports celebrities in Minneapolis, but celebrity is celebrity. I've had more than one problem with them, especially from *Truth Seeker Confidential*. So it's good you said nothing, and he didn't have a camera. Not that I saw, anyway. Otherwise, he'd probably have you all over the Internet by tonight. Come to think of it, I'm surprised he *didn't* have a camera guy…"

I don't know why that's so strange, but Higgs knew best about this stuff.

As Jeff settled at my feet, curling around my ankles, I wondered aloud, "Should we alert Suzanne they've found her? You know, so she can protect herself?"

Higgs gave a sarcastic chuckle, unfolding his napkin and placing it in his lap. "I don't think she'll be unhappy about it. In fact, it wouldn't surprise me if she was the one who tipped them off. She's certainly not afraid of the spotlight. I bet her motto is some press is better than no press. But I'd definitely shoot Knuckles a text and at least make him aware. He doesn't deserve the kind of trouble this could bring. I'm sure that Ben guy followed Suzanne from the police station, and Knuckles *is* the one who drove her to his place. What I don't understand is why this Ben didn't just ring the doorbell and try to get her to talk. It's not like they have any shame when it comes to getting a story, and they're definitely not shy."

The waitress approached and took our order, leaving us in a moment of silence as I thought about what Higgs said. Would Suzanne really capitalize on her husband's death for two minutes on the news?

Then I mentally slapped myself. Duh. Of course she would, so I quickly sent Knuckles a text to be on the lookout for nosy reporters, just in case.

Higgs splayed his long legs out in front of him and stretched his arms. "I'm going to give my old contact at *Truth Seekers* a call and check on this guy. I don't know if she's still there, but it can't hurt to ask about him. Anyway, what did he want to know?"

I sat up straight, unable to contain my excitement. "Oh! I forgot. Did you hear any of what he said at all?"

He planted his chin on top of his fist and shook his head. "Nope. Not a word. Enlighten me."

As I gave Higgs the instant replay and the waitress brought our order, my mind whirred with questions I intended to ask Suzanne the moment I could get my hands on her.

"So a prenup, huh?" Higgs asked, taking a big bite of his eggs over medium.

"Yep. According to that Ben Adams, if they divorce or Suzanne was unfaithful, she got nothing. I don't know if it's true, but that's definitely a motive for murder."

Higgs wiped his mouth with the paper napkin. "It definitely is, but how do we know he's telling the truth? Maybe he was just fishing for some answers. They bluff and bait all the time just to trip you up, Trixie."

I nibbled on a strip of bacon and typed the magazine's name into my search bar, and right on the front page, there was a picture of a very alive Agnar entering an attorney's office, clear as a bell. Hendrix, Timmons, and Barr, Attorneys at Law, was the name of the practice, and they very definitely were divorce attorneys. The headline read: *Is This The End of The Road for The Scream Queen and Her Latest Victim?*

I held up the phone and showed Higgs. "The article is dated last week. So if Suzanne's the kind of person to Google herself, and she read this article and found out Agnar was seeing a divorce lawyer, she could have tried to kill him last night as a way to prevent him from divorcing her, right?"

He cut up a thick sausage with his fork and nodded. "Yep. That's true, and her asking us to help her find who did this to Agnar could all be an act. It's what she does for a living, after all. But we have no confirmation on that story. Who knows if Agnar really was seeing them about divorcing Suzanne or they're just friends who have the occasional lunch together? *Truth Seeker's* a rag mag. You can't always believe there's even a grain of truth to what they publish. It's all geared toward sensationalism."

Sighing, I dabbed some butter on my toast. "We need to talk to their friends and find out what they know about their relationship. Surely their friends would know about whether their marriage was strained. If Lucinda's her BFF, she'll likely know something."

"Agreed. The question is, will she share that with us?"

"So the next move?"

"Next, we go to the hotel where they're staying and find them, see if they're willing to talk to us."

I ate a forkful of fluffy scrambled eggs. "And if they're not?"

"We rough 'em up and make 'em."

I blinked and cleared my throat. "Seriously?"

"Would you still be game if I said yes?" he asked, giving me a serious look.

I squirmed. This wasn't going the way I'd thought it would. I didn't want anyone hurt, but what did I know? I'd watched enough police shows to know sometimes that's what officers of the law did to get answers.

And Higgs had been undercover in a gang…he probably wasn't above doing what it took to play a part. Gang members aren't gang members because they host pinochle games and ice cream socials.

But then I caught Higgs grinning that infectious grin. Sometimes when he smiled the way he is now, I had to wonder how he'd gotten away with playing the part of a gang member in the first place. He didn't look like he had a mean bone in his body, despite his size and stature.

"You're having a laugh at my expense, aren't you?"

Higgs laughed, throwing his napkin down on his plate. "Absolutely, Sister Trixie. My roughing-up days are officially over."

I made a face at him and waved to the waitress for our check. Time was wasting and we needed to make a move. "I don't believe you ever roughed anyone up. Not for the sheer pleasure of it. So save that for someone who's buying what you're selling."

Yet, instead of laughing at my joke, his face went a little dark momentarily before he put on that familiar smile that hides all his ills. "I appreciate the faith."

I dug around in my purse for some cash, leaning back in the chair and letting the warm sun settle on my face. "It's beautiful today, isn't it, Higgs? Close your eyes and inhale. You can smell the river, hear the seagulls."

His chuckle was light. "I like the way you appreciate the little things, Trixie. We, as a whole in society, don't do that enough anymore."

I smiled and reached down to give Jeff a small piece of bacon. "The little things are all part of the puzzle that is the big thing."

"Profound—"

"I swear, I couldn't believe it!" a guy said excitedly from two tables away where a group of four men sat, his loud voice catching our attention. "He was riding along, buck naked of course, and out of nowhere, this car comes around the corner and sorta runs right into him. Like, bam— almost T-bones him! Turns out the driver just grazed his bike, but man, dude rolled off that bike like he was a stuntman in some movie. If he hadn't been naked, I might have thought they were filming some action flick. But check this—just as me and Jones go to help the guy, he gets up, grabs his bike, hops on, and takes off like a flippin' champ. I'm tellin' you, man, he's my hero!"

Both Higgs and I hopped up from the table, but I was the first to make it to the group, my heart racing. Solomon, for all his babbling, had been right. They had to mean Agnar.

How many naked men on bikes who get hit by cars were hanging around Portland last night?

In my excitement, I approached them with less courtesy than I'd care to admit. "Excuse me? I don't mean to eavesdrop, but am I correct in saying you saw one of the naked bike riders hit by a car last night?"

The man who'd told the story gazed at me from his place at the table, suspicion lurking in his clear gray eyes as his friends all stopped talking.

Higgs came up behind me and placed his hands on my shoulders, leaving the warm imprint of his palms against my thin T-shirt. "Sorry, guys. I'm Cross Higglesworth, and this is my friend, Trixie Lavender. She owns the tat shop over on Peach Street. You know, the new one that just opened a month or so ago?"

One of them slapped the man who'd told the story

on the back. "Aw, yeah! Inker-something, right? The one where we saw that crazy good-looking redhead. Remember, dude? We saw her out front last week, sweeping off the sidewalk. Almost made me want to get over my fear of needles and get a tat. Man, is she ever smokin'—"

The man who saw Agnar's accident jabbed his friend in the ribs and shot him a cross look. "Shut up, Jones. She probably works with this lady. Sorry. My friend forgot to tuck his knuckles in before he got here. Sometimes they drag on the ground."

I held out my hand to him and smiled, ignoring his apology. Coop *was* smokin' and he was a man. Maybe he was a little misogynistic and overzealous, but everyone was a work in progress.

"Sorry, miss. Forgot myself for a minute there," he apologized, looking down at his feet.

I skipped right over the inappropriate nature of his comment and introduced myself. "My name's Trixie, and yes, I own Inkerbelle's Tattoos and Piercings. Forgive the intrusion, but did you say you saw a naked man hit by a car last night?"

He bobbed his head with enthusiasm and shook my hand with a firm grip. "I'm Darren Thomas, and my big mouth friend is Abel Jones. Yes, we saw the guy get hit—or *grazed* is probably a better word. I mean, he didn't ram him or anything, but it was still impressive the way the guy on the bike got right back up. We were going to help him, but he got up like he wasn't just plowed down and rode off on his bike, healthy as the day is long. It was the craziest thing I've ever seen."

"And the car?" I asked. "What happened to the car?"

Darren shook his head. "Took off. Never stopped, never even bothered to check on the guy. People these days, right?"

Yeah. People.

However, that accounted for the crooked tire on Agnar's bike, but did it account for his death? I hate to admit it, but excitement swirled in the pit of my stomach. This was a genuine lead.

"Where did it happen?"

Abel thought for a second and then he said, "Royal Street. Right by the bike repair shop."

"Did anyone else see anything?"

Darren shook his head. "I don't remember seeing anyone else. The ride was winding down at that point, with just a few stragglers. I don't even know how someone got a car past all the barricades. But I definitely don't remember anyone else around."

Darn. "Did you happen to see the make and model of the car? Did you see what color it was? Or can you describe who was driving?" I asked.

His sigh was ragged as he ran a hand through his thick reddish-brown hair. "Crown Vic, for sure, black, but the windows were tinted. Looked like an old police car, but I couldn't see much more than that. How about you, Jones?"

"Same," his friend said. "Do you know the guy on the bike?"

"He was a friend of a friend," I replied. In the interest of keeping things simple and avoiding any misinformation getting out, I figured I'd better be careful.

"Was?" Darren said, his voice wavering ever so slightly.

Higgs spoke up then, removing his warm hands from my shoulders. "Unfortunately, I'm sorry to report, he died."

Abel's face showed genuine remorse. "Aw, man! I'm really sorry. I swear to you guys, he looked fine when he got up and took off. Otherwise, we'd have called the police. Shoot. I'm really, really sorry."

"Do you think you'd mind speaking to the police?" I asked hopefully. "I'm sure this information would be helpful. Can I put them in touch with you?"

Darren bobbed his head. "Sure-sure. We'll help however we can. We didn't see much, but I guess it's better safe than sorry."

"Thanks, guys. Appreciate the help. Stop by the shop if you're ever interested in getting a tattoo. I'll give you a discount for being so helpful."

I took their information to forward to Tansy while Higgs looked down at his phone with an odd expression.

As we weaved our way back to the sidewalk with Jeff in tow, I frowned. "Everything okay?"

He held up his phone. "Tansy sent me this about an hour ago. Must have missed it while we were chatting

up your friend Ben. Read. It's the results of the preliminary coroner's report."

I scanned the text from Tansy and gasped.

"Agnar Stigsson's official cause of death: Rare,
unidentified toxin introduced through the
bloodstream."

CHAPTER 10

e'd dropped Jeff off at Higgs's apartment, all the while, my wheels turning. As we entered the hotel where the group was staying, I was still a bit shocked.

"So basically, that means someone poisoned him?" It certainly explained why there were no marks on his body, none visible to us anyway. The bike had taken most of the impact.

Or maybe we hadn't seen any marks because of the position he'd been lying in on the ground. Maybe the side that had taken the hit was the side we couldn't see?

Higgs stopped in the middle of the swanky marble and gold lobby and shrugged. "It could mean any number of things. But you read it yourself, that's all Tansy's giving me, and she only told me because that's what she's releasing to the press. She just gave it to us a little earlier than the news outlets. If she knows what the toxin is, she's not telling me."

"And there's definitely foul play because they'd already labeled his death a murder last night. The police knew something was wrong then. So I call she poisoned him. Oh!" I said excitedly. "Bet she put it in his water bottle! Did you see it on the sidewalk? They collected it for evidence."

"I'm sure they'll test the water bottle, but it's obviously not something common like arsenic because Tansy called it a rare toxin. And you've already determined Suzanne killed him? Jump the gun much, Sister Trixie?"

I sighed. "Okay, that's fair, but it's what makes the most sense."

"Or you're making an assumption based on emotions," Higgs reminded me as we waited for the group to come downstairs.

I gave him some good old-fashioned side eye with a hand planted on my hip. "Whose side are you on, Higgs?"

"The victim's. You're Knuckles's friend and Suzanne did him wrong way back when. Stands to reason you'd lose objectivity because you don't like her."

Then I had to try harder to remain objective. I couldn't let my feelings get in the way of sending this woman back from whence she came. "You're right. I'll work harder."

"Keep that in mind, because here they come."

Suzanne had given us permission to talk to her friends as a way to help her, but it wasn't looking good for her after what we'd learned this morning. I wasn't even sure where to begin. Yet, I couldn't help but wonder, if Suzanne had anything to do with Agnar's death, why would she give us free reign to speak to her closest friends about her and her marriage?

Higgs leaned down toward my ear as the group crossed the threshold of the lobby, looking tired but very stylish in their clothes. "You know, we never talked about the rules of this pseudo investigation."

"It's not pseudo. It's really happening." I was being facetious and I knew it, but I had a feeling Higgs's rules were going to cramp my style.

He cocked a raven eyebrow at me. "Okay, our *unofficial* investigation then. We haven't talked about the rules."

"Well, I'll tell you what, ex-undercover cop, we'll have a nice chat about them after we talk to Suzanne's friends, okay?"

"Good enough for me. Because I have them, you know. Some rules."

"I'll just bet you do," I said on a chuckle. I got the impression Higgs had always played by the rules until he was forced to make some of his own.

If getting his help meant following the guidelines he set forth, it was fine by me. Er, mostly. I mean, how do I know? I've only done this once, and I failed most of the way until I got lucky.

This was all new to me. I didn't want to make promises I couldn't keep because I didn't yet know how far I was willing to go to catch a killer.

"Everyone looks so much different with their

clothes on, don't you think?" he asked with a saucy grin.

Rolling my eyes, I walked toward the group of Suzanne and Agnar's friends, their eyes weary, their body language telling me it had been a long night. I stuck my hand out to Edwin Garvey—the letch who'd put his number in Coop's phone.

As he approached and took my hand in his, I had to admire how well preserved he was, too. He was easily in his late forties, maybe even closer to fifty, but he looked healthy and fit, and the clothes he wore showed he was fashion forward.

Lucinda was the second to reach me, her prettily made-up eyes filled with tears. "We just saw the news! I don't understand what a rare toxin means? None of this makes any sense!"

I reached out for her hand, too, and gave it a squeeze. "I'm so sorry, Lucinda. I don't know any more about the specifics than you do at this point."

Edwin sighed, bringing my attention squarely to him. "Edwin Garvey, correct?"

He smiled that handsome smile, his beautifully sculpted face tan and lean. "Friend of the very luscious Coop, correct?"

I swear, it was all I could do not to give him a good dressing down for being so obvious and bold about his interest in Coop. I wondered if his money allowed him this sort of behavior—as though he'd been granted a hall pass for debauchery because his bank account was fat.

Instead, I looked him dead in the eye with a blank expression. "It's Trixie Lavender. I own the tattoo shop you were all going to visit last night before your friend was found dead."

Myer Blackmoore let out a wheezing sigh, his eyes bleary. "I can't believe Agnar's gone. We've been friends forever. I don't know what I'll do without him."

My smile was warm with sympathy as I reached out and took his hand, which was cold and clammy. "I'm so sorry, Mr. Blackmoore. I'm sure Suzanne told you we're here to try and help. Oh, and by the way, this is Cross Higglesworth, an ex-police officer. He was kind enough to agree to help me."

Cross shook hands with everyone and pointed to a round table and chairs in an atrium to the left of the lobby. "Shall we sit? You all look like you could stand to take a load off."

Without waiting for an answer, he led everyone to an atrium filled with small groupings of carefully tended plants, where the sun poured into the glass ceiling and the atmosphere was bright and cheerful.

As we all settled, I noted Grady Hanson looked quite put out, judging by the frown on his face, while everyone else appeared at least open to helping us.

"First, as I said, I'm Trixie Lavender, and I'm so sorry for your loss. I know the police kept you until the wee hours of the morning—"

"Which begs the question, why did Suzanne ask you to talk to us, Miss Lavender?" Grady grumbled, placing a beefy hand on his round belly as he settled into his chair. "Why doesn't she just let the police handle this?"

Lucinda Ferris was the first to reach over and swat Grady on the arm, the bracelets lining her wrist clinking and sparkling in the sunlight. "Hush, Grady. Suzanne already told you why she asked them to help. The more help the better. Didn't you hear Suz? This man's an ex-police officer, and the ex-nun caught a killer once. It's like hiring a private detective without having to pay the bill. Stop being so negative and answer the woman's questions so we can get this over with. I want to go back home, and we'll never do that until the police clear us all. So please, ask away, Tipsy."

I gritted my teeth and silently cursed Suzanne. "It's *Trixie*, and I'm not here to give you grief, Mr. Hanson. Believe me when I tell you, I'm no expert when it comes to police matters and solving crimes. I'm just helping out a friend of a friend. How could I say no to a woman who just lost her husband so suddenly?"

Myer, his face so gaunt for someone who made food for a living, nodded vigorously. "She's right, Grady," he reprimanded, turning to look at me. "You're absolutely right. I'll help in any way I can, Miss Lavender, if for no other reason than to extend the courtesy to Donald, who I'm sure has his hands full with Suzanne. So please, ask me anything."

Grady still grumbled, but he nodded his head along with everyone else, leaving me feeling less intrusive. Thus, I dove in, folding my hands in front of me.

"I'll warn you, I might ask a question or two that

offends you. But I'm not doing that to be cruel or to ruffle your feathers. I'm just hoping to understand what happened to Agnar. I'm hoping to see something the police haven't. Is everyone all right with that?"

As everyone nodded once more, I watched their faces and, but for Grady, they all appeared concerned.

"So as you know by now, the police are labeling Agnar's death a homicide by a rare toxin. Any thoughts on what exactly that might mean?"

Their blank stares told me they were either really good liars or they truly didn't know.

Higgs cleared his throat. "Did you see him eat anything unusual? Take any medication? Perhaps a drug?"

"Agnar was a health nut. He didn't take any kind of recreational drugs, and I didn't see him eat anything but a kale and quinoa salad yesterday before we headed out for the naked bike ride," Myer said, his eyes angry, but the anger wasn't directed at Higgs. His expression said he was angry at the situation.

That out of the way, I decided to poke around their friendship with Agnar. "Let's begin with how long you've known each other. Have you all been friends for very long?"

At that, Myer smiled, his eyes distant. "As I said, Agnar and I have been friends for a very long time, but it was only in the last two years we decided to begin this quest to bike around the world. You wouldn't understand because you're still so young, Miss Lavender, but there comes a time in your life when you can't keep the weight off no matter what you do, especially in my line of work." He clapped a hand to his middle, which didn't have an extra ounce of flesh, by the by. "So I happened upon a cycling experience in Peru near Machu Picchu when I was there to judge a contest for up-and-coming chefs. I enjoyed it so much, I mentioned it to Agnar, and it sort of took off from there. Soon, we were traveling all over the world, attending cycling events—the more outrageous, the better—which is what led us to the World Naked Bike Ride. Our motto was you only live once," he said on a melancholy laugh.

I dunno. I could live a million times over and still never want to ride a bike naked. I'd wondered last night about how comfortable they'd all been nude. Maybe it was the shock of finding their friend dead, but no one appeared terribly concerned. Though, I guess that's what body positivity is all about.

"So you've all known each other for a long while then?" I wanted to know how well they knew not only Suzanne but each other.

I remember Stevie once telling me if a suspect is backed up against a wall, they're likely to give up even their own mothers to keep from being caught. I wanted to see how tight their bond with Suzanne really was.

"Agnar and Suzanne have been married for almost a decade, so I've known her at least that long. Lucinda's always been with Suzanne, traveling from set to set as her stylist and good friend. Edwin and Grady have both been around as long as I have."

Everyone nodded again, assuring us the information Myer gave me was correct.

"I already know what you do for a living, Myer. Knuckles... Er, Donald filled me in. But what about you, Edwin?"

Edwin lifted his square chin and nodded his head. His face was somber, but his eyes twinkled as though mischief was on his mind. He rather reminded me of a younger George Hamilton—very tan, very good-looking, very charming, and not at all ashamed of his love of beautiful women, if the way his eye kept wandering to the young waitress in the adjacent bar was any indication.

"I am— Er, *was* Agnar's business partner. As I'm sure you already know, Agnar was an art dealer. We dealt in rare and exotic paintings, sculptures, etcetera. You name it, if someone called and needed to sell, we were the people to do it. I was the mouthpiece; he was the one with the head for business. I love to travel, so I handled the dealing portion of the business. He was a homebody and didn't like to be too far from Suzanne unless she could come with, so he handled clients and booked appointments. We rounded each other out rather well."

Why didn't I find it surprising that Edwin was the mouthpiece? "And how long have you been in business together?"

Edwin blew out a breath and paused as though he were mentally counting. "About thirteen years now."

Higgs tapped his finger on the table as Edwin's eyes

began to stray to the group of women at the desk. He boldly eyed their backsides like the letch he was. "Do you know of anyone who might have taken issue with Mr. Stigsson? Any angry clients?"

Edwin brushed invisible lint from his crisp black button-down shirt. "We didn't deal drugs, Mr. Higglesworth. We dealt in art. That means lots of rich people who want to own a Francis Bacon so they can show all their other rich friends all the things their money can buy. There aren't a lot of angry rich people. Not angry enough to kill Agnar, certainly."

Holding up my phone, I pointed to the story I'd found about Agnar. "So let me begin with this article I saw on *Truth Seeker Confidential*. Are you aware the magazine did a story about Agnar last week? They claim he went to see a *divorce* attorney."

Lucinda's eyes instantly clouded over as she toyed with her statement necklace, a large hoop full of colorful balls. "I'm aware of it. Suzanne showed me."

I sat up straight and leaned forward. "So she knew he'd gone to see a divorce attorney? Was their marriage truly in trouble the way the article alleges?"

Myer's thin shoulders, encased in a gorgeous tweed blazer, slumped. Frankly, he looked miserable, and I felt horrible for him. "Agnar was dreadfully unhappy. He wouldn't say why, but he did tell me things had gone awry."

Higgs ran a hand over his chin and leaned forward in his chair, his eyes sharp as tacks as he scanned their faces. "Did he say what happened or why they were unhappy? Do you know the root of his discontent, Mr. Blackmoore? Or any of you, for that matter?"

Myer's face went dark and distant, his chocolate-brown eyes watering. "He didn't talk much about it. Agnar was a private man, even with me, and we've been friends for years. I only know he was unhappy. Yet, if he saw a divorce attorney, I wouldn't be surprised."

Out of nowhere, Lucinda dropped her palms on the table with a slap, making us all look up. Her hair, like glass it was so smooth, swung forward, grazing her chin as she rose to her feet. "Stop, Myer. Just stop!" she hissed. "You know as well as I do, Suzanne's a no-good, lying cheat!"

Higgs and I looked at one another, and I wondered if he was wondering the same thing I'd been.

Was Suzanne too blind to see even her own friends thought she was a snake?

CHAPTER 11

*E*dwin instantly reached over and soothed Lucinda with a bronzed hand to her arm. "Loose, take it easy, honey."

Was he saying that to shut her up or because he was concerned she looked as though she might have a seizure?

But she yanked her arm away from him and shook her head with a furious motion. "I will not take it easy, Ed! I'm not going to lie for her—not when things are as serious as they are! Listen, Trixie, Suzanne's not a good person, and I say that even though I truly love her. She's never satisfied, and it's never her fault. Agnar was good to her—*really* good to her. But you know Suzanne. There's always a bigger pot of money to be had. The problem is, she was getting a little long in the tooth and her pool of prey is growing smaller by the minute."

Okay, so here's the thing—even her own friends

don't like her. I'm not so sure I should be tarred and feathered for feeling the same way. And I said as much with my eyes when I looked over at Higgs, who appeared as flabbergasted as me.

"Lucinda speaks the truth," Grady Hanson confirmed, rolling his tongue along the inside of his cheek. "Suzanne's needy and insensitive, and she can't begin to fathom the world doesn't revolve around her."

Again, I looked to Higgs, who was likely thinking what I was thinking. Lucinda sounded very bitter, even though Grady backed her up. Maybe she was jealous of Suzanne's beauty? Tired of living in her shadow? You know, the usual wallflower/prom queen BFF complex? I couldn't figure out why she'd stayed with Suzanne so long if she didn't like her.

"How long have you been friends with Suzanne?" I asked quietly.

Lucinda pursed her crimson lips. "I've been her stylist for what feels like a hundred years, and at least a hundred men have passed through her doors in that time. I love Suzanne. I really do. I *swear* I do. She's opened doors for me that never would have opened without her. We've been friends since college, and I've followed her all over the world. But I know her almost better than I know myself. I'm calling it as I see it, and if the goal is to help find out who murdered a man as nice as Agnar, I'm going to tell you the truth, and the heck with Suzanne's snowflake feelings. Agnar deserved better than her. Period."

Higgs drew in a breath, his wide chest heaving. "So

you knew they were having trouble in their marriage, Miss Ferris?"

Lucinda's lips thinned in distaste as she looked down at her perfectly manicured hands. "I know what I saw, and I saw Suzanne treat him poorly all the time. She'd stay out till all hours of the night, ignore his phone calls and texts. She belittled him at every turn. Yet he pandered to her constantly. All she had to do was say jump and he would ask how high, when he was really the one who needed someone to be there for him."

I didn't understand what that meant. So I asked. "Meaning?"

Myer reached over and grabbed Lucinda's hand, giving it a squeeze. I didn't know if it was a signal for her to stop talking or if he was consoling her. "Meaning, Agnar had asthma. He had a horrific attack about a month ago and it landed him in the hospital, but Suzanne was too busy on a set somewhere to come be with him."

Lucinda scoffed, her eyes narrowing. "Too busy? Is that what we're calling sleeping with the grip on set? Then sure. She was too *busy*."

Okey-doke. There was definitely some bitterness there. After hearing Lucinda, I'm surprised it wasn't Suzanne who'd ended up dead.

"It's true," Grady confirmed in a quiet voice, scratching his bushy, graying beard. "Suzanne ran around behind his back with whoever she thought had the most money."

"A movie grip hardly qualifies for the *Forbes* richest list, Miss Ferris," Higgs pointed out.

She barked a sarcastic laugh, her eyes narrowing. "Please. That quickie was only to confirm she's still got it. It was a throwaway in her trailer on set, and likely only happened because he couldn't shut up about how much he loved her in *Machete Man*, and how he'd been a fan ever since. He fed her enormous ego, nothing more. She forgot about him the way she does everyone else, two seconds after she threw him out of her trailer. That's always how that scenario plays out."

Now I inhaled, deeply. Talking to Suzanne's friends wasn't going the way I'd expected. The tension was thick enough that I could cut it with a knife. But this was for Knuckles. I wouldn't stop until I was satisfied I'd gotten everything I needed.

"So were you all aware she'd get nothing if Agnar found out she was unfaithful or if she wanted a divorce? Is what the article said true about the prenup?" I looked to Myer, his oldest friend, for the answer.

"It is," Myer confirmed in a hushed tone. "Agnar had those precautions put in place because his first divorce was so ugly. He lost everything to his ex-wife, and he waited a long time to remarry, but it wasn't without the sting of a reminder from his first divorce."

"Are there any children involved?" Higgs asked.

Edwin shook his dark head. "No children for either of them."

"As if Suzanne would ever allow her body to be

sullied by carrying a child," Grady scoffed on a huffy breath.

Yet, Myer gave him a scalding glance. "Knock it off, Grady. She's an actress, and she's not the first woman who doesn't want to have downtime from her career to raise children. She's many things, but don't crack wise about her resisting procreation."

"No, of course, Myer. You're right. I should thank her for not bringing someone like her into the world," Grady said, each word like a bullet shot from a gun.

"Grady!" everyone whisper-yelled at him, making him slump in his chair, his thick lips thinning.

As I typed some of this information into my phone, I liked Suzanne less and less, if that was at all possible. But if I wasn't a fan, Grady *really* wasn't going to head up her fan club.

Finally, I asked, "Then I guess the question is, did Agnar know she was running around behind his back? Did he suspect?"

"Well, obviously, Miss Lavender," Edwin drawled, looking very bored. "He did see an attorney, didn't he?"

Edwin, for all his attractiveness, was rubbing me the wrong way. I didn't like his condescending tone. "I meant prior to his visit to the attorney's office, *Mr. Garvey*. Lucinda's statement suggests Suzanne has always played around. Did he know she'd been doing this for the entirety of their marriage—or did he happen upon this information just recently?"

Myer steepled his hands in front of him, his eyes distant. "I think he first realized, or at least finally believed what he saw with his own eyes, when we were in Brazil. I was visiting a restaurant I was opening there, and Suzanne was doing one film or another—"

"*Born in Blood 2*," Lucinda spat with a roll of her eyes, repositioning herself in her chair.

"Yes. That's the one," Myer confirmed with a nod of his dark head. "There was a lot of talk amongst the crew about Suzanne's behavior, and unfortunately, Agnar overheard some unsavory rumors on set one day. Of course, I did my best to reassure him they were just that—rumors, because we had no confirmation. But the seed had been planted. There was no turning back from there."

Nodding, I typed the information into my phone. "And when was this, Mr. Blackmoore?"

"A year ago," Lucinda provided, though she appeared less angry now. "If you want schedules or dates and times for Suzanne's shoots, events, whatever, I have them all on my tablet for at least the last five years. I can send them to your email, if you'd like."

"That would be terrific," I said. And then I made mention of something that had struck me as Lucinda talked about Suzanne. "It sounds like you were more than just her stylist, Lucinda. You sound more like a personal assistant."

Her laugh was filled with wry sarcasm as she crossed her arms over her chest. "I was whatever she needed me to be whenever she needed me to be it."

Gosh, to be so angry with her friend, to have harbored so much resentment for so long…again, I was surprised Suzanne wasn't the one who'd ended up dead.

Cupping my cheek in my hand, I asked, "Do any of you have any idea who could have done this to Agnar? Did he have any enemies? Any altercations, big or small? Could it have been someone Suzanne had an affair with? An overzealous fan? Everything counts at this point, even something you might have thought insignificant at the time could mean something."

"I can't think of a stinking thing, Miss Lavender," Grady groused, obviously growing weary of my questions. "Suzanne was Suzanne. We accepted that Agnar loved her with blinders on. She came with him as part of the package."

When everyone else shook their head in the negative, I decided it was time to ask if I could sift through Suzanne and Agnar's room, and whatever was left of her belongings that she hadn't packed and had Higgs cart around as though he were her personal butler.

"Do any of you have access to their room? I promise not to touch anything. I just want to take a peek. Maybe something will jump out at me."

"The police have already done that, Miss Lavender," Myer assured me. "They were here early this morning, rummaging through both their rooms. As far as we've been told, they've cleared both rooms. Though, Suzanne hasn't officially checked out."

"Sometimes a fresh set of eyes, uninhibited by certain restraints, can help," Higgs said, surprising me.

I thought the last thing he'd want me doing was rifling around in their personal belongings.

Lucinda dug around in her beautiful handbag—one that matched her equally beautiful outfit perfectly. "They had separate rooms. I have Suzanne's key because we had an adjoining room."

That information made me pause. "They didn't stay in the same room? Is that normal for them as a couple?"

Lucinda's sigh grated its way out of her lungs. "They never stayed in the same room. Suzanne said, and I quote, 'Agnar's wretched wheezing from his asthma keeps me from getting a restful night's sleep.'"

Man, one more nail in Suzanne's coffin. She certainly wasn't the most compassionate of women.

I reached over and took the key card, looking to the group once more. "Does anyone have Agnar's room key?"

"No, but I'm sure I can get you one," Myer offered. "I own one of the restaurants in this very hotel. They've been very accommodating. I'm sure it'll be no problem." He made a quick exit to the front desk, his steps long and sure.

I pushed back the cushioned chair I'd been sitting on and stood up, extending a hand to each of them. "Again, my condolences to you all. I'm sorry your trip to Portland turned out so poorly, and I hope I didn't make it worse by being so intrusive."

After we all shook hands, Lucinda, being the last of the bunch, pulled me off to the side and whispered, "If you ever want to tap into the absolute gorgeousness that you hide behind your thrift-store clothes, give me a call. I'd be happy to do it pro bono, if only to see what it does to your insanely good-looking cop friend's insides."

I gave her a confused look. First, these were a brand-new pair of jeans, thank you very much, and my T-shirt was clean as a whistle.

"Oh, no, Miss Ferris. You've misunderstood. We're just friends. Neither of us is in the market for a relationship."

Or at least I didn't think we were. I mean, I sure as heck wasn't. I was still trying to figure out how not to be a nun.

"Says you," Lucinda said on a sly smile and a wink. "You didn't see him looking at you the way I did." She gathered up a strand of my very unremarkable shoulder-length hair and held it up to the sunlight. "You have lovely hair, thick and shiny. With the right stylist and coloring, a little lip stain, and you could be a whole new woman. But do yourself a favor and get rid of the blue streak. It does nothing for you. Either way, the offer stands."

"Thank you," I murmured. At least I think I was supposed to be thanking her. Do you thank someone for insulting your clothing?

Myer brought the key for Agnar's room to us and once more offered his help if we needed him, and with that, they were gone, leaving Higgs and I to wander off to the elevator in stunned silence.

When the elevator dinged, we hopped inside, and all at once, my thoughts came rushing out. "Wow. With friends like that, who needs enemies?"

Higgs leaned back against the wall of the elevator and shook his head with a grim smile. "She's some piece of work, huh? If I didn't know better, I'd think *she'd* be the target, not Agnar. By all accounts, he was a good guy. Even her best friend liked him better than Suzanne."

I jabbed a finger in the air to make my point. "See? I told you she wasn't very nice. They just confirmed my assessment."

Higgs grimaced, his expression skeptical. "Yeah, but did she murder Agnar? I have my doubts."

I snorted, pinching my temples with my fingers. I had a real headache on the way. "Well, she must have known what they'd say about her wasn't going to be favorable. She can't be that blind, can she? If she did murder her husband, she's hiding in plain sight after that conversation—which takes chutzpah."

"I think we both know Suzanne's got plenty of chutzpah, but it's suicide to think you can pull something like that off. I vote Suzanne's not our killer."

As the elevator stopped, I checked the time on my phone. I had an hour to look through their rooms before I needed to get to the shop. "I vote you're the expert. Now, I'll take Agnar's room, you take Suzanne's? If there's anything left in there, that is. I can't imagine after five bags worth of luggage there's much to sift through, but for the sake of thoroughness, we'd better leave no stone unturned."

"Agreed," Higgs said as he stepped out of the elevator and headed down the long, plush hallway, stopping two doors ahead of Agnar's. "Text me if you need me. Oh, and Trixie? For the record—I like the blue streak in your hair."

"You heard her?" I squeaked, hoping the floor would swallow me whole.

"Just the tail end about your hair."

I hid my face, but my cheeks were on fire as I slid the card in the door and stepped inside the cool interior of Agnar's room, grateful for the air conditioning to ease my embarrassment. Higgs's comment after Lucinda's words had me in a tizzy I couldn't afford to be in right now.

Sighing, I took a deep breath and cleared my thoughts, taking a peek around the opulent room. At first glance, Agnar's room looked neat as a pin. The bed was still made with foil-covered candies left by the maid service on the pillow. He had but one suitcase and a lone briefcase, and by the looks of it, the police had already tossed both.

I knelt down and eyed the jumbled pile of clothing, but I didn't see anything unusual, just a bunch of underwear, a pair of jeans and a couple of polo shirts. I was afraid to touch anything, but then, the police had already been here and done their jobs. There probably wasn't anything left to sully.

So what would be the harm if I picked through his clothes and his briefcase?

I can talk myself into almost anything, and that's exactly what I did as I plucked his clothing up one by one and dropped them on the floor until the suitcase was empty. I was doing this for the good of my cherished friend Knuckles, who I didn't want to see sucked into the web of infidelity and deceit that is Suzanne.

Next up, the bathroom. Crossing the room with its thick white carpet and deep mahogany furniture, I entered the bathroom and flipped the lights on, where I encountered a marble sunken tub with jets, a long vanity, and two sinks with gold faucets. There wasn't much to see but the guest shampoos and soap, as yet unused. I imagine the police had taken any personal toiletries to test them for this toxin.

Darn.

I caught a glimpse of my defeat in the lighted mirror and lifted my hair, holding it up to the lights. There was nothing gorgeous about my hair, or me, for that matter. In fact, if I were to rate myself objectively, I was quite average, and I was at peace with that.

I shook off Lucinda's comments. I didn't need a makeover, and I didn't need to focus on my insecurities. I needed to catch a killer, and so far, I was having no luck.

My phone buzzed, signaling a text. I pulled it from my back pocket and went to the door to open it for Higgs.

He poked his head inside, wrapping his hand around the door. "Anything?"

"Not so far," I said, crossing the room to open up Agnar's briefcase. "You?"

Higgs shook his head and walked toward the big window overlooking Portland. "Not a darn thing. I think what we saw last night really was all of it."

Popping the briefcase open, I doubted we'd find anything in it, simply due to the fact that it wasn't locked. Clearly, Agnar wasn't concerned about anyone finding anything of importance. But I was going to give it a look-see anyhow.

As I lifted the papers inside, I discovered I was right. There wasn't anything but a receipt for a chain for his bike and some kind of modern art magazine.

With a ragged sigh, I said, "Nothing. You check the nightstands and I'll look under the bed."

Kneeling, I lifted the heavy white duvet cover, throwing it up over the bed and using my phone's flashlight app in order to see, but again, I came up with a big fat zero. My shoulders slumped in defeat as I sat cross-legged on the floor and closed my eyes.

"Being an amateur sleuth is hard, ex-undercover police officer, Cross Higglesworth."

Higgs came and sat next to me and patted me on the shoulder. "I know, Nancy Drew. But you asked some great questions back there."

I gave him an odd look. "Ya think? I had no idea what I was doing. I feel like I should have asked more or gone deeper."

"You pretty much covered it all, Trixie. It's some of the same stuff I would have asked if I were officially investigating Agnar's murder."

I leaned forward and pressed my forehead to the mattress, my tension headache worsening "I'm sorry I got you involved in this, Higgs. I wasted your entire morning for nothing. Go on. Call me a fool. I can take it."

He laughed his husky chuckle. "You're not a fool for trying to help Knuckles. I want to help him, too."

Okay, enough feeling sorry for myself. Did I really expect to solve this mess in a matter of hours, being the novice I am? I mean, we still don't know who Jack The Ripper was, and that happened over a hundred years ago, right? So why would I know who'd killed the naked biker one day into an investigation? I was becoming as bad about instant gratification as anyone in this day and age of technology.

So, in essence, suck it up, Lavender.

I popped my eyes open—and that's when I saw it.

It was just a small discoloration against the snow white of the mattress, but it was enough to grab my attention. I pushed the heavy mattress upward a little and my eyes widened.

"There's something in there—under the mattress!" I almost yelped, hopping up. "Help me lift, please, Higgs?"

Using two hands, Higgs hoisted the mattress up and right there, for all to see, were what at first glance looked like pictures. I grabbed at them, just some flimsy pieces of printer paper, and held them up.

My eyes went wide with shock and my stomach rumbled in discontent. "Holy ham and cheese!"

Higgs let the mattress go and moved closer to me. "What is it?"

Blood coursed through my veins in my excitement as my hands shook. "Well, well, would you look at that." I flicked the paper with my fingers as I danced around. "Somebody wasn't telling us everything downstairs, because Suzanne was definitely having an affair—and someone in the group knew it."

I almost couldn't look at the pictures of Suzanne and her lover *in flagrante*, they were so graphic, but it wasn't as though I hadn't already seen them naked, right?

Yet, disgust filled my gut at how flagrantly they'd avoided telling me everything—right to my face, no less.

Higgs frowned, the wrinkles in his forehead growing deep. *"What?"*

"Suzanne was having an affair all right, and this proves it. I can't believe the police didn't find this!"

Higgs's eyes narrowed. "We know she's had several affairs, Trixie."

"But we didn't know she was having an affair with this guy!"

"Is that who I think it is?"

"If you think it's Grady Hanson!"

CHAPTER 12

*B*ack at Inkerbelle's, I sat in my tiny, pale blue office with Higgs while customers filed in and out, fretting over what to do next.

We'd called Tansy and told her what we found, and she was sending over an officer to pick up the pictures I now regretted touching due to leaving behind my fingerprints. Oh, and the curt what-for Tansy gave me for sticking my nose in where it didn't belong.

I'd offered to keep Higgs out of things, but he insisted he'd take the heat with me. Still, we'd found a vital piece of evidence the police had missed, and now we had to address what to do with the information.

I sat back in my office chair, a gift from Knuckles, and ran a hand over my tired eyes. "So, Suzanne was having an affair with Grady Hanson, and he talked about her like she was the devil incarnate. Oh, I'm so angry with him right now, Higgs!"

Higgs sat across from me at my small desk I'd

purchased at a used office supply store, looking big and bulky in the small space, but his smile was full of sympathy.

"Well, he did that for obvious reasons, Trixie, to keep suspicion from landing squarely on him. He obviously wasn't going to offer up the information, especially not in front of his friends."

I held up the pictures of Suzanne and Grady, no longer concerned my fingerprints were all over them. "So who took these pictures and why?"

"It could be a lot of things. Agnar could have hired a private detective, for instance, but it's obvious he knew Suzanne was unfaithful and he wanted to prove it."

"How do we go about finding that out?"

"A search on his credit cards, bank accounts."

I threw my hands up in the air as I stared at the picture of all of us at Inkerbelle's opening. Knuckles had it framed for me in a beautiful teak, all of us smiling and excited.

"Like I have access to some mysterious database. I don't have that kind of advantage, Cross Higglesworth."

"But the police will. It'll be some of the first things they look for while investigating the state of Suzanne and Agnar's marriage."

I gave Higgs a coy look and all but twirled my hair. "Do you have access to a database like that?"

He cracked an amused smile at me and shook his head. "Not anymore."

Then another thought occurred to me. "Or maybe

someone was blackmailing him? Though, that doesn't make a lot of sense, does it? I mean, why would he care if Suzanne's hijinks were plastered all over the Internet? He didn't seem like the kind of guy who could be hurt by a scandal. He deals in rare art. I'm not sure that involves much scandal unless we're talking fake paintings. His life wasn't very public the way Suzanne's is."

Higgs nodded. "Also true."

"And then there's Grady. I'm sure he didn't want Agnar to find out he'd been having an affair with Suzanne, but it makes no sense he'd kill Agnar. The way he talked about Suzanne would make you think he wanted *her* dead, not his friend. So, if we consider him as the killer, what's his motive?"

"Jealousy? Maybe he was jealous of Agnar and wanted Suzanne all for himself? Getting rid of Agnar would make that possible. Yeah, he talked a lot of smack about her, but that doesn't mean he wasn't putting on a show for us."

"Well, that'd make sense if not for the fact that he didn't have to kill Agnar to get her—all he had to do is promise her a buttload of money. Clearly, that's what motivates Suzanne, and she's obviously not afraid of divorce—she's done it three times. Plus, Grady's as rich as Agnar was. He didn't need Agnar's money—which *Suzanne* would get if he died before he could divorce her."

"Also a fair assessment. I don't see a motive on his part, but I've seen people kill for less."

"Then answer me this, why in all the whys in all the

wide-wide world would Suzanne give us the green light to go and talk to her friends if she was playing around with one of them? Is it me, or is that just crazy risky?"

Higgs toyed with a pen on my desk, scratching something out on a sticky note. "I think she was counting on the fact that Grady didn't want to be found out any more than she did. So, she rolled the dice, figuring he'd keep his mouth shut, and she was right. I'm convinced she didn't know Agnar was on to her, and if she's not afraid of divorce, your theory about her killing him is off. If we listen to your theory, she'd just go off and find another husband, right?"

I puckered my lips and jabbed a finger in the air. "But! Lucinda said it best, Suzanne's getting long in the tooth. It's harder to find a man, especially in Hollywood, if you're over the age of twenty-five. Her looks won't last forever. As it is, she's surely been through a medical procedure or two to keep that youthful glow and all that breathy charm only goes so far."

"Then why wouldn't she just leave Agnar and run off with Grady? No murder required," Higgs countered.

Higgs had a point, darn it. "Maybe he didn't want her for anything more than…what's it called these days? A sidepiece? And another thing," I all but yelped. "What kind of people do this to someone they claim to love? If you think I'm angry with Grady, I can't even begin to tell you what I want to do to Suzanne. How will I face her tonight at Knuckles's house?"

Higgs shot me that warning look he'd given me once or twice when I'd griped about some social injustice or another. "You'll do it because you have to, and you're angry because you're emotionally invested, Sister Trixie. You care about Knuckles. Feelings get in the way, which is why I discussed rules. Number one rule, don't get emotionally involved."

I rolled my eyes so hard, I think they touched the back of my brain. "Oh, sure. That's fine for the ex-police officer to say. You've been taught to compartmentalize. But I'm no officer of the law, and I want to die at the thought of Knuckles finding this out about Suzanne and Grady. He's been especially melancholy lately, Higgs. I told you, I think he's missing Candice more than usual."

"But don't you think he already knows she's a cheat, Trixie?" Higgs asked in a hushed tone. "Isn't that why they broke up all those years ago?"

My sigh was one of aggravation and disgust for Grady and Suzanne and the mess they'd made. "Yes. It's why they broke up. But he attributes that to her youth. I know in his heart of hearts he was hoping she'd changed since then. Sad panda to find she's the same old Suzanne, and now, I have to tell him."

"After Tansy sees those pictures, you won't have to tell him a thing. Suzanne will be back down at the station faster than you can say torrid affair. Believe me, Trixie, he'll find out."

My stomach twisted into a tight knot, knowing this news would sadden him. "But I don't want him to find out like that, Higgs, I don't want to see him hurt. Oh! I could just—"

A knock on the door interrupted us and made me get a grip on my anger. "Come in," I called out, feeling utterly miserable at the prospect of telling Knuckles this new information. I didn't want him to hear it from the police. I wanted to be there for him.

I was surprised to see Oz, the young officer I'd met the night before, poke his head around the door with a smile. "Miss Lavender. Detective Primrose sent me to pick up those pictures."

I smiled at him and tucked the pictures into a manilla envelope. "Trixie. It's Trixie, please, and good to see you again, Oz."

Higgs stood and held out his hand to him. "Oz, pleasure as always. Trixie, I've got to get back to the shelter, but I'll drop back in here before closing. Tonight's your late night, right?"

I rose, too, stretching my arms upward with a small yawn. It had been a long morning. "Yep. I'll be here till nine or at least Coop and Goose will, but if you need me, just pop on over to the house. So either way I'll see you later. Oh, and Higgs?" I said, pausing with a smile of gratitude. "Thanks again."

"You bet," he said on a wave as he headed out.

"Sooooo," I drawled as I handed the pictures to Oz. "Anything new on the Stigsson case? Like an as-yet-unidentified rare toxin being identified?"

His handsome, youthful smile ratcheted up a notch. "Nothing I can share with you, Trixie."

"So that means there's something new?"

"That means I plead the fifth."

"Don't they only do that on TV?" I teased.

"Nope. I do it in real life all the time."

I laughed, coming around the desk to prepare to head out and handle things in the shop. "Well, if you ever feel like sharing anything, anything at all, I'm your girl."

He tucked the pictures under his arm and lifted his chin, gazing down at me with his light blue eyes. "Speaking of sharing, would you like to share a cup of coffee with me sometime?"

At first, I think I misunderstood. Remember, I'm not exactly hip to the ways of dating and such. In fact, I'm woefully out of touch. "I never share my coffee. Coffee is sacred 'round these parts," I joked.

He barked a laugh, flashing his white teeth when he grinned. "No. I meant maybe we could grab a cup *together* sometime."

I frowned and cocked my head. I didn't mean to, of course, but why would he want to have coffee with me? I'm the single-most boring person ever.

He must have noted my confusion, which incredibly astute on his part. "I'm asking you out on a date, Miss Lavender. Nothing formal, just some coffee and conversation."

Ahhh. Oh, dear. A real live date? No. I didn't think that was a good idea. But then, as of late, I prided myself on coming from a place of yes, and a new experience was a new experience, right?

"As friends?" I asked, then felt all kinds of fool.

A date meant he was interested in being more than my friend, I suppose, but I hadn't looked at him in that way. As a nun, I didn't spend much time with men unless they were priests, and I certainly hadn't even begun to explore how I saw a man if he wasn't wearing a cassock.

Awkward.

His smile was genuine and sweet. "That's as good a place to start as any."

"Then it's a date. Er, I mean, coffee. It's coffee." Ugh. I was such a dolt at this.

"That it is." He held up the envelope and waved it. "I'll be in touch. For now, I'd better get these back to the station. See you soon, Trixie."

"See you soon, Oz."

As he took his leave, I pressed my hands to my cheeks, once more flaming hot in embarrassment.

How, I ask you, will I ever actually go on a real date with anyone ever if I can't even accept a simple offer of coffee without treating it as though it's a lifelong commitment?

Maybe there's a dating handbook for dummies like me.

Note to self, after you find Agnar's killer, look up how to date when you've been a nun your entire adult life.

∿

"*T*rixie, lass, you're falling asleep at the wheel. Surely this can wait until the morrow? Is this woman really worth so much time and effort?"

My eyes popped open at Livingston's words as I found myself hunched over my laptop, sifting through the eighty-bazillion pictures of Suzanne on her Facebook page. "Knuckles is worth the time and effort, and no. It can't wait until tomorrow, Livingston. I have to figure this out."

"Or?" he coaxed.

"Or Suzanne's going to be calling you a filthy pest until she finds somewhere else to go."

"Oh, that foul woman is a disgrace to humankind, Trixie! The nerve of her to say such a ting about me."

I winced. Livingston and Suzanne had endured a small altercation this afternoon while we were all at work. She'd attempted to move him to another room because she was sure she'd get some rare disease, and as a result, he'd nipped her. As you can imagine, that hadn't gone over well.

Especially when Knuckles had defended Livingston —good naturedly, of course, but nonetheless, it angered Suzanne.

Now, as we sat around our living room waiting on word from Knuckles, who was with Suzanne at the Cobbler Cove Police Station for more questioning about those pictures—and had absolutely refused to let us come wait with him—we were still trying to piece together anything that would help us with Agnar's death.

"Well, in her defense, you did bite her, Livingston," I reminded, plumping one of the many pillows on our couch and readjusting my position.

Livingston ruffled his feathers, his glassy gaze fixed on me from atop his perch in our tiny living room. "I most certainly did not. My mouth opened and happened by chance to graze her lily-white skin. That's not the same ting as a bite, darlin'. Had I bitten the saucy hen, she'd have known it for sure, dumplin.'"

"You were rude, Quigley Livingston," Coop chastised as she padded across the hardwood floor and dropped down beside me on our puffy, white-and-cream-colored couch, freshly showered and in her pajamas. "No one *happens* to open their mouth when someone's arm is near it. You did it on purpose, and don't lie to me. It's wrong to lie."

Livingston sighed and swiveled his head. "Call if what ya will, lass, that woman's unbearable. For someone who's mournin' her husband, she's on the phone an awful lot with her friends. She never shed a tear all day long, but she sure dilly-dallied the day away."

"You know, Livingston," I remarked, fighting a yawn. "I didn't think of the benefits of having you around while she's at Knuckles's house. I'm almost glad you opted to stay home instead of greeting your adoring fans at the shop. She has no clue you can talk and understand her. That means you can keep us abreast of what she's up to."

Why hadn't I thought about the fact that we had our own little spy much sooner?

"You know what she's up to, lass? No good, that's what. I tought she'd lose her blessed mind today when she discovered that Angus froze all their accounts and she couldn't buy some fancy pair o' shoes. All because, get this, she spent ten-thousand dollars on some day spa or another—or so she claims."

I stared at Livingston, aghast. "His name is Agnar. And holy baloney! Agnar froze their accounts?"

Livingston straightened his spine and spread his wings. "If I heard the shrew roight, he did."

I gripped the top of my laptop and stared at her picture. "Wait…did he do it *before* they left LA? Did she say?"

"I only heard her tell someone on the phone that she had no money and her husband was the reason."

Coop crossed her long legs, tucking them under her. "Money is the root of all evil."

I patted her leg and smiled wearily. "Apparently, according to her friends, so is Suzanne," I said on a giggle. "But to find out Agnar cut her off financially before all this happened is telling. I wonder if she knew *he* knew about her affair before they got here or after? Or if she knew at all? Which begs the question, why would she let us poke around in her life if she knew we'd find out so many awful things?"

Nothing was frustrating me more than that bit of information.

"Trixie?"

I stared at the computer screen, the words and images becoming blurry while we waited on Kunckles. "Yes, Coop?"

"We need to have a conversation," she said, folding her hands in her lap, meaning this was serious.

I twisted my upper torso around to look at her. "About?"

"About your possession."

"Now? What we need to be doing right now is finding a killer. My evil insides can wait."

Coop's finely arched eyebrow shot upward. "You're avoiding the discussion."

I suppose I was, and how very astute of Coop to notice. "I think you're right. That's very perceptive of you. What's on your mind, Coop?"

"I've been doing some research about demonic possession, and I found out a thing or two I think you should be made aware of."

My mouth was suddenly dry as my eyes avoided hers and focused in on the gorgeous painting of a vase filled with pink peonies and white roses hanging on the wall next to our half bath.

"What do I need to be made aware of?"

"We need to find out your demon's name."

"So we know what name to use to address his invitation to my birthday party?"

Coop threw her head back, a la Joan Collins, and

laughed long and fiendishly—for my benefit, of course —to show me she was still working on accurately portraying human emotions.

When she lifted her head, she asked, "You're joking right now, aren't you?"

"Yes. And your Joan Collins laugh keeps getting eviler by the minute."

"Too much still?"

I held up two fingers and smooshed them together. "A little."

She sighed in resignation. "Darn. I can't seem to get that right. And stop avoiding the subject by veering off into my wish to blend with humans. Your demon has a name. We need to discover what it is."

I let my head fall back on the couch, closing my eyes with a sigh. "Because?"

"Because once we can address it by name, we can demand it release you."

That made me sit up ramrod straight. "Where did you find that out?"

She grabbed my laptop and typed in a web URL, bringing up a site called SatanRules.org. There wasn't much to it but a scary picture of a grim reaper with the face of a skull and a couple of tabs, one of which listed demons.

Coop clicked on the tab and brought up another page. She highlighted a paragraph. "Here. It says in order to draw the demon out, you must call it by its name, Trixie Lavender. It's the only way to exorcise it. You are a descendant of Adam, and God gave Adam dominion over all things. By extension, knowing the name of the demon will give you power or, as it states, *dominion* over the demon, and then maybe you can control it. But it's my understanding it takes great will to force the hand of the demon."

My head popped up, and suddenly I was totally awake. I knew most scripture like the back of my hand, and I knew all about what the Bible said about exorcism, and some examples of what occurred during an exorcism.

What Coop said is technically true, if you believe what's been handed down over the years, but in all this time since I'd left the convent, I'd forgotten entirely how the Bible relates to my possession. And I fully admit, it's simply because I don't want to hit this head on. I just want it to go away, and I know realistically, that's not going to happen.

But Coop was a demon herself. Surely, she must know about a hard-and-fast rule like this? "Coop, you're a demon. Have you ever heard of something like this?"

She stared at me, her eyes blank. "If this rule truly exists, a demon of my rank and status wasn't made aware of such. But then, I wasn't a part of possessions. I only know they exist. I can't vouch for whether calling the demon by name will rid you of him, but surely it's worth looking into."

Surely.

I shrugged my shoulders. "I'm game if you are. I don't know how we find out my demon's name, but next time he shows up at the barbecue, let's give it a whirl."

She shook her long finger at me. "You're being flippant."

I grinned. "I am. Nice word. I thought you were still on the letter A in your quest to absorb the entire dictionary. How'd you get to F so soon?"

"I got bored, so I skipped around a little to alleviate the monotony."

Chuckling, I turned to Livingston. "Hey, pal, you've got a new job."

"Oh, magnificent. Does it involve peckin' a churlish woman's eyes out?"

"Livingston," I warned, slipping from the couch to place my laptop on the counter of our small island/bar top, overlooking our amazing white and navy blue kitchen. This kitchen—this glorious, shiny-steel-with-miles-of-snow-white-quartz-countertop   kitchen—made me wish I could cook.

"Yeees?" he drawled.

"Promise me you won't hurt Suzanne. I realize she's difficult, but I won't have her hurt on my watch. Also, if I'm not around to protect you, you could end up at Animal Control. You're lucky you didn't today. So knock it off."

His sigh grated, whizzing about the room. "Fine, lass. What is this job you're yammerin' about?"

"Spy on Suzanne. Listen to her phone calls, watch what she does online, do whatever you have to in order to find us a lead in this so she'll go home. Deal?"

If Livingston could roll his eyes in sheer irritation, he'd roll them so hard at me right now. Instead, he conceded. "Fine. But I expect to be rewarded with cookies. Oreos, I'll thank ya kindly. Double Stuf's. The whole package, not just some namby-pamby crumbs because my cholesterol levels are at stake."

I laughed out loud. "Deal. Oreos it is—*a whole package.*" My phone vibrated on the counter and I grabbed it, hoping against hope it was Knuckles, sending us a text to tell us he was on his way home so we could go to sleep.

But it wasn't. It was Higgs.

As I read the text, I gasped in surprise for the second time today.

Spoke to my contact at the stationhouse. More news they've kept close to their chests since the preliminary reports. The coroner found the broken tip of a dart embedded in the left cheek of his butt-ox laced with a toxin. Toxin remains unknown at this point.

Someone had shot the poor man in the rump to kill him?

Well, if ever there was a kick in the pants, Agnar sure had gotten his.

CHAPTER 13

I put my head on my desk at Inkerbelle's and yawned wide as I waited for Knuckles to arrive after his very long night at the police station. We'd all fallen asleep on the couch, hoping to at least see him, but his text told us Suzanne was beside herself and almost inconsolable (I know you find that as shocking as I did) by the time the police were done with her.

Still, they'd released both her and Grady after questioning them with the warning they shouldn't leave town just yet.

So Knuckles did what he does best—he nurtured her. He made her a cup of her special tea, tucked her in, and texted that he'd see us in the morning. And here it was, morning, and here I was, waiting on Knuckles before I went and had a chat with Grady Hanson, who'd been suspiciously unavailable when I'd requested to meet with him just after we'd found the pictures of him and Suzanne.

Today was a different story. Today, he'd agreed to meet me in the hotel lobby. But for right now, I needed to see my friend and reassure myself he was all right.

While I waited, I'd scoured everything I could find on Suzanne on the web. I went to every single fan forum, every single fan site where there were pictures of her at horror conventions or movie premieres or charity events. In essence, I'd been all over the place, trying to find anything suspicious anywhere with anyone and I came up empty-handed.

I lifted my head and closed my laptop, resting my forehead on my hands and shut my eyes, grainy and tired as though I'd been chopping onions, and all the while, Agnar's cause of death swirled in my head.

What toxin was deadly and unidentifiable? I'd done a Google search, but rare toxins were a dime a dozen and there were a million ways to use them as deadly weapons. If it wasn't the obvious, like strychnine or cyanide, it could be hemlock or your garden-variety arsenic.

After further texting with Higgs, I found out the broken tip of the dart found in Agnar's hide is definitely what killed him, but as yet, whatever substance was used hadn't been revealed—nor had they found the dart responsible for killing him.

And still, there was no word on how the police had received the news Darren gave me yesterday about the Crown Vic. Both Abel and Darren were kind enough to drop by this morning and let me know they'd given statements to the police (although, I think Abel really only wanted to get a glimpse of Coop). So I knew for sure the police had the information.

But if my gut isn't exactly as finely tuned as Coop's, it sure was standing at attention when I considered the hit and run had to do with Agnar's death as much as the dart with this mysterious toxic substance.

But how? And why? Did whoever was driving the car shoot the dart at Agnar, successfully land it, then get distracted and hit his mark by mistake? From the eyewitness testimony, nothing was mentioned about anyone rolling down a window, something you'd surely have to do to shoot a dart, nor does the way Agnar was hit by the car lend to that line of thinking.

It would have been impossible for the car driver to land a dart if he was facing Agnar when he rammed into his bike. So were the two incidents totally unrelated and was my gut just a big, fat stinker?

"*Who killed you, Agnar?*" I whispered out of desperation into my empty office. "If you're up there, and you can hear me, send me a sign, would you? I know this isn't very nice, but your wife is really mean. Though, you already know that, don't you? I just want her to go home and leave Knuckles in peace. I'm worried about him and how vulnerable he seems to be around Suzanne. So lend a girl a hand, would you? Some divine intervention would be most appreciated."

"Trixie?" Knuckles entered my office, his enormous frame dwarfing everything around him.

I hopped up from my chair and scooted around the desk to give him a welcoming hug, my relief very real. He wrapped me in his warm embrace and ran his knuckles along the top of my head. Then he held me at arm's length. "You okay, Trixie girl? Who were you talking to?"

I smiled up at him and his tired eyes. "Oh, just myself. You know how that goes. I'll always get the answer I want."

His rumble of a chuckle even sounded tired. "Very true."

I patted his back and asked, "You okay? You had a really long night, my friend. What can I do to help?"

"You could give me the day off? I'm pretty darn fried, kiddo. I can't do all-nighters like I used to. My party animal left the building a long time ago."

I smiled in sympathy, my heart hurting for him. "Of course you can have the day off, Knuckles. Goose and Coop are here, and you know how business early in the week goes. It's always slow. No sweat."

He pinched my cheek with his beefy fingers. "Thanks, little lady."

Gosh, this moment wasn't one I'd been looking forward to, but I had to ask. "So, you heard about Suzanne and Grady?" I asked on a wince, hating everything about this pending conversation.

Knuckles stiffened, his massive chest rising and falling as he let out a breath. "I did. I heard you were the one who found the pictures, too."

I looked down at my sandals. "It was just dumb

luck. I'm sorry, Knuckles. I had no idea I'd find something so incriminating…"

He shrugged his wide shoulders. "It's not your fault, kiddo. You did the right thing."

Did I? If hurting my friend was "doing the right thing," I'm not sure I *want* to do the right thing. "How do you feel about what I found?"

His hands suddenly dropped from my arms and rested at his sides. "How am I supposed to feel?"

Oh, dear. *Proceed with caution, Lavender. Danger, Will Robinson, danger.*

"I don't know, Knuck. I'm just checking in with you. If you want to talk about what's going on, I'm always here… I guess that's just something I need you to know."

"What's to talk about?" he asked, as though Suzanne hadn't been memorialized in pictures, wrapped up in a naked clinch with Grady Hanson.

I bit the inside of my cheek. I'm almost never at a loss for words, but I was surely struggling right now. "Okay, let me start again. Suzanne asked me to help find out who killed her husband. I did that, *am* doing that, as a courtesy to you—because you're my friend. I didn't mean to find what I found yesterday. I wish I hadn't found what I found yesterday—"

"Why? Because you bein' an ex-nun and all means mistakes aren't allowed?" he cut me off, his words stiff.

My inhale was sharp. It was as though he'd slapped me in the face, and I had to fight to keep the sting of tears at bay. I knew he was lashing out because he felt defensive about Suzanne and any residual feelings he had for her. It was a kneejerk reaction when you know you can't help the emotions you have for someone who isn't very nice, but I think he had the past and the present mixed up. I had to keep that uppermost in my mind.

"That's not what I'm saying at all, and I'd like to believe you know *that* much about me. But there's a distinct pattern with Suzanne's behavior here, Knuckles. Surely you can see that?" I asked, tiptoeing into the murky waters of our friendship.

His resolve was like steel as he folded his arms. "I see a woman who made a mistake—a pretty big one. I also see a woman who's lost her husband and sorely regrets that he knew about that mistake before he died. Maybe she had an epiphany and didn't have the chance to tell him? People do that all the time after something tragic happens. That's what I see. What do *you* see, Trixie?"

I see an actress who's vying for an Academy Award in her mind while she plays you for a fool.

That's what I wanted to say, but of course, I didn't.

With my heart in my throat, I said, "I see that you're angry, but I'm not sure why. If you'll tell me, I'll try and fix it."

Knuckles looked me directly in the eye, and I couldn't read the emotion, but I'm pretty sure it was disappointment. "I'm not angry, Trixie. I'm disappointed."

Yep. I'd read his eyes right. "In?"

"You're an ex-nun, Trixie. Of all the people in the world, I'd have thought you'd be the first one willing to forgive someone for their indiscretions, sins, whatever you people with religion call it. She's apologized, but I guess that's not good enough. Instead, you're being judgmental, and I'm here to tell ya, I don't like it." Then he shook his head, his eyes full of confusion. "Bah! I don't know, Trixie. I'm all mixed up inside. I just need some time."

Had the floor opened up and swallowed me whole, I couldn't be more stunned. Tears burned my eyes. I'm sure—no, I'm *certain* Knuckles was reacting defensively because of his old feelings for Suzanne, and they're mixed up with his longing for his life partner. The wires are all crossed, but man, those words hurt.

So I did the only thing I could do. Give him time. I stood on tiptoe and kissed his cheek. "I'm sorry you feel that way, Knuckles. You take the day off, go home and get some rest. I'll see you later."

"And think about what you're sayin', man," Goose said from out of nowhere as he pushed the door to my office open wide. "You go on and get yourself some sleep, because I'm not gonna have you talkin' to Trixie like that, and I have to believe it's 'cause you're tired and frustrated. Trixie's good to us. She cares about you. I know I said I wouldn't say anything more, but I'm not gonna stand around and listen to you hurt the kid's feelings. That flippin' Suzanne's bad news, and you can either like it or lump it. Now go home and get some rest, you big lug, and don't come back till ya got your pants on straight."

Goose pointed to the door of the shop with a knobby finger, his eyes, lined by age, flashing with anger.

Knuckles narrowed his gaze and thinned his lips but he didn't say a word. He turned on his heel and marched toward the door, his back stiff, his boots the only sound as his footsteps echoed in the shop.

I didn't realize I'd been holding my breath until I let out a long exhale. Goose put a comforting hand on my shoulder. "You all right, kiddo?"

No. I wasn't all right. I wanted to sit down and have a good cry, but I nodded. "I will be." I just needed a minute to get past the shock of Knuckles's hurtful words.

Goose lifted my chin with his index finger and winked, his wrinkled face turning upward in a grin. "You listen to me. Knuck's not in his right frame of mind right now. He's a little stupid when it comes to that woman—always was until she proved she was nothin' but a headache. He'll kick himself later for what he said to ya, but no way I'm gonna let him forget who his real friends are and talk to ya like that. You let him cool off, but don't take what he said to heart, kiddo. He's only known you a short time, but he loves you girls like his own. He just needs some time to come around. Okay?"

I think that's the most Goose had ever said to me in one conversation, but you know what they say about the silent ones. You have to look out for them because when they finally speak, it's usually profound.

On impulse, I threw my arms around his neck and squeezed him hard, hiding my face against his shoulder in an effort to cover up my tears. "Thanks, Goose," I whispered. "I know you're right. I'll just have to give him some time."

He leaned away from me and pinched my cheek. "Good girl. Now go on and talk to that dirtball who was messin' around with Suzanne so we can get this mess over with and send her packin'."

"You think I should keep investigating?" I squeaked in disbelief.

I was ready to pack it in to save my friendship with Knuckles. I didn't want to find anything else out about Suzanne that could damage our relationship.

"Yeah, I do. The faster you find out who killed that wretched woman's husband, the faster she'll be gone. You wait and see. She's usin' Knuckles because she has nowhere else to go, but the second she does, she'll be outta here lookin' for greener pastures. That means, you have a murder to solve so I can be the first one standin' in line to wave goodbye to her."

I fought a giggle. "Then I'd better get to it." I squeezed his hand, my heart full of gratitude for his soothing words. "Thanks again, G-Man. You're awesome," I said as I squeezed past him to head for the door.

"Just you remember what I said, and be careful, kiddo. Me n' Coop'll hold down the fort."

I waved my hand over my shoulder, avoiding looking at Coop, who was busy tattooing a young woman's ankle.

Mostly I avoided looking at her because I didn't want to cry, but the moment I stepped outside, I inhaled the warm air and tears began to fall down my cheeks.

Knuckles's words had cut me to the quick, and I know they shouldn't. I know he's all caught up in the wonder of Suzanne and her dilemma. He was a protector. A nurturer. But if nothing else, his adoration made me that much more determined to find out who killed Agnar.

If what Goose said was true, and she really would head off to greener pastures, I had to act fast.

Because you can bet your bippy, I'll be the second person in line right behind Goose, waiting to wave goodbye to her.

CHAPTER 14

I rose from my seat and stuck my hand out to Grady Hanson and he took it, though his eyes held guilt that was clear as the day is long.

"Mr. Hanson, thanks for seeing me," I said as we sat once again in the atrium of the hotel.

"Did I have a choice?"

"You did. You could have said no," I said, my tone showing my displeasure.

"And have those two nags on my back about owing Suzanne?" he said, referring to Lucinda and Edwin. "Not on your bloody life. So what can I tell you that I haven't already told the police? It's obvious I'm not guilty because they let me go. I have a solid alibi."

My eyes honed in on his round face. I wasn't here to mess about. My resolve was steadfast. I wanted Suzanne to go home. The only way to do that was to figure out who killed Agnar. "I'm not interested in your alibi, Mr. Hanson. I'm interested in your relationship with Suzanne."

He snorted and took a sip of his whiskey straight. "We didn't have a relationship. We had a fling, and when she found out I wasn't going to marry her, she ended it. End of story. There's really nothing more to it than that."

Well, that was a surprise. "*She wanted to marry you?*"

He leaned back and crossed his ankle over his knee, the smooth blend of the material of his trousers shimmering in the sunlight. "She wanted to leave Agnar, but Suzanne doesn't do things without a soft place to fall. She was setting up her next paycheck by vetting me, but I'm not, nor will I ever be, interested in marriage, and certainly not to Suzanne."

My next question wasn't going to go over well, but I had to ask. "Forgive me for saying so, but you seem to feel nothing but contempt for Suzanne. Why would you have an affair with her and ruin a longtime friendship with Agnar if you didn't even like her?"

He barked a sarcastic laugh, rolling his glass of whiskey in his hand, the amber liquid sloshing. "*No one* likes Suzanne, Miss Lavender. She's a dreadful person. As to the affair? She came to me one night in distress over her relationship with Agnar—it was turning into a total mess. Our encounter became physical, as some do when one person is distraught. It really does work the way they say it does. It just happened. Anyway, like I said, Suzanne doesn't do anything that isn't calculated to within an inch of its life, and she knew if Agnar divorced her, she'd lose everything. She needed a backup plan. But she was sorely mistaken if she thought I would be that backup."

Phew, that was ice cold. I didn't understand these people. Not at all. What motivates the rich isn't the same as what motivates the rest of us.

"But she'd lose everything if she was unfaithful, too."

"Which is likely why she used every charm she possesses to woo me," he said dryly. So dryly it was as if he were talking about a financial transaction, not a human being.

"So why didn't you tell the police or even me about the affair? Why hide it?"

"Listen, Miss Lavender. I don't want to ruin her. She's a horrible person, but then I'm no better, am I? I indulged in her charms behind my friend's back, and what fine charms they were," he said in a hushed, almost creepy tone, as though he weren't recollecting in broad daylight. "I don't want to see her destitute, is what I mean. I didn't want anyone to find out because infidelity is part of her prenup. Why shouldn't she get Agnar's money? And now that he's dead, where else would it go? If his lawyers found out she'd been unfaithful, she wouldn't get a dime from his estate. I just didn't want her for my wife—or for anything more than I already had, for that matter. So I didn't tell you out of courtesy to her. If it meant she could keep Agnar's money; it's no skin off my nose."

How generous. This guy was some piece of work.

Yet, his words, so distant and removed, sent a chill skittering along my arms and spine.

"So you had no idea Agnar had hired a private investigator? He didn't confront you or say anything to you about your affair with Suzanne?"

For the first time since we'd sat down, he actually looked remorseful. "Now *that* is unfortunate. No. I had no idea, but who can blame the man? His wife's a leech. He wanted out, and he was smart enough to know when the jig was up, but smarter still for protecting himself. Suzanne's the fool here. She signed the bloody prenup, knowing full well she'd never be faithful."

You know, as much as I didn't like Suzanne, I think Grady was a close runner up to my disgust. He'd cheated with his dearest friend's wife. These two people deserved each other.

I swallowed my distaste, forced my face to remain expressionless (thanks, Coop!) and asked, "When did the affair start?"

He gave me a bored look and tipped the last of his whiskey into his mouth. "In Brazil. We were all there for Myer's restaurant opening and of course, as you know, Suzanne was filming some vile movie or another where she pretended to be an actress of worth. It was right after we'd visited the set—in the jungle, mind you. Hotter than Hades, it was. Dreadful place full of all sorts of deadly plants and snakes. Couldn't wait to get out of there."

"So it didn't last long then?"

"Not terribly, no. I'm a loner, Miss Lavender. I don't

like messy entanglements or lengthy interactions. I have plenty of those with my clients as an investment banker. They're trying enough. Forgive my brutal honesty, but I got what I wanted from Suzanne, and that's really all there is to tell you."

He began to rise, but I placed a hand on his arm. "One more thing, Mr. Hanson. Any idea who the private detective Agnar hired is? A name? Anything? Maybe someone he might have used because one of you used their services?"

"Not a clue, but I can tell you this, whoever he was, kudos to him for being so slick, because I never once suspected." And then he chuckled, appearing quite pleased with himself.

I thought all sorts of horrible thoughts about Grady Hanson, said some horrible words in my mind, too, and then I decided it was time to talk to the source.

Suzanne.

She probably wouldn't like it, and neither would Knuckles, but they'd just have to get over that. Now more than ever, I wanted these people to go back to where they came from.

❧

"*I* told you, darling, I think I'm going to stay here with Donald—at least until I have to be on set, and maybe even afterward. He's not my usual victim, but if we're being brutally frank, the pickings are getting slimmer at my age. I'm big enough to admit that. Donald has enough money to satisfy me until I can find a more suitable situation. His house isn't the style to which I'm accustomed, but it will suffice for now. Though, I'd like his frumpy nun to find somewhere else to live, and her strange friend. They're nothing but a nuisance, always lurking around here. Not to mention that filthy owl they have for a pet who almost took my arm off. But I'll find a way to get rid of them. I always do." She paused and sighed. "Oh, I could just kill Agnar for leaving me with nothing!" Then she giggled. "Forget I said that, he's already dead, isn't he?"

My jaw literally dropped to the floor, unhinging at the words I was hearing, coming out of this woman's mouth. I'd left the despicable Grady Hanson and decided to come back to Knuckles's and pin Suzanne down and make her answer my questions. I'd have to find a way around Knuckles, but I figured I'd deal with that when it happened.

For now, my laser focus was on Suzanne, who happened to be sitting out in the sun on Knuckles's gorgeous deck lined with pots of hydrangeas, peonies and a mix of impatiens and marigolds, in her festive pink bikini, sipping a cocktail and chatting on the phone with heaven only knows who.

Knuckles had left a note on the fridge for Suzanne that read he was going off for a ride to clear his head, but he'd be back to cook her dinner—which only made me angrier.

Maybe it was the idea that he still wanted to cook for this lying, cheating, money-hungry gold digger and she didn't deserve him, coupled with her words on the phone, but I'm going to admit, I plum lost my mind. Right out on the deck in broad daylight.

Coop, on her lunch hour, was off in the guesthouse kitchen with Livingston, who I desperately wanted to talk to about Suzanne's day, but not before I got my hands on this infernal woman.

As I approached her, she all but rolled her eyes, as though I were nothing more than a nuisance rather than the person who was trying to find out who'd killed her husband.

I don't like admitting it, but I snatched the phone out of her hand and threw it on the patio chair's teal-blue cushion. I'm sure there was some steam coming out of my ears at this point, but I'd lost myself in my ire.

Suzanne cupped her hand over her eyes, her gorgeous skin glowing with the beginnings of a light tan, and frowned her outrage with as much over exaggeration as her face could display. "Who do you think you are? How dare you!"

Looking down at her, I narrowed my gaze until she was a tiny pinpoint of my fury. "I'll tell you who I am, Suzanne. I'm *Donald's* friend, and not a chance in this lifetime I'm going to let you take advantage of him. Understood?"

Her gaze was coy, almost sickly playful. "I don't know what you mean, dear."

Oh, she knew what I meant. She knew exactly what I meant, but I made peace with saying it out loud.

Clenching my fists, I fought the urge to gather her up by her teeny-tiny bikini strings and shake her but good.

Sitting on my haunches, I leaned in close to her, my eyes narrowed. "I heard what you said on the phone. *Every. Word.* Just so we're clear, Suzanne. I don't know what you're up to. I don't know if you're involved in this mess or you're just playing another one of your parts, but if you toy with Knuckles, you'll have *me* to deal with. Understood?"

Wow. Look at me go all gangster. But I couldn't help it. I'd watched Knuckles fall for this woman's "poor me" act, tripping over his own feet to keep her and her demands happy, and it was beginning to wear thin. So thin. I wouldn't have this dreadful excuse for a human being, who used people up for the sheer pleasure of using them, hurt my friend—especially not after what I'd just heard.

He deserved better. Maybe he was in a bad place emotionally, missing Candice and all, or maybe Suzanne brought back memories he was too blind to see weren't as great as he'd like to remember them being, but by heck, he wasn't going to get sucked into her baloney on my watch. Not if I could prevent it from happening.

Her eyes narrowed to tiny blue slivers as she pushed her untamed hair over her shoulder. "Are you threatening me, Sister Tipsy?"

I stared her down, my eyes glued to her beautiful face. "Yep. You bet I am. And it's Trixie. *Sister Trixie*

Lavender, thank you very much. Try and keep that straight, and while you do, make it your business to finish up whatever needs finishing and go home the moment the police say you're all clear."

Her smile was sly, her sharp jaw held high. "But Donald already invited me to stay."

My right eye began to twitch, the muscles in my arms and legs flexing with tension. "And I'm *uninviting* you. I don't suppose you'd like me to pass on that phone call I just heard, would you?"

She dismissed me with a wave of her hand, making me even angrier. "He'd never believe you. Never in a million years," she drawled.

Listen, I don't get red-hot angry often, but this cruel, ugly-on-the-inside creature was making me see all shades of red. "Really? You don't suppose he'd believe an ex-nun over a has-been actress who cheated on her husband with one of his closest friends and once broke his heart? Wanna give it a shot and see who comes out on top?"

I knew after my conversation with Knuckles, he was still firmly in Suzanne's camp, but I had to bluff her in order to smoke her out.

And then she did it. She one-upped me. Played her trump card with a flourish.

Sighing wistfully, she threw her legs over the side of the lounger and rose to her dainty feet. "Oh, I think after tonight, he won't be able to resist me, *Trixie*. Because I have plans for my sweet Donald this evening.

The kind of night that involves only adults, if you know what I mean…"

Then she winked and turned on her heel, pushing her way through the French doors to head toward the living room, essentially dismissing me.

Okay, look. I know I'm a nun, and nuns are supposed to be patient and kind and not lose their tempers.

But please be fair if you chose to judge me. Nuns are as human as you or anyone else and, if we're honest, Suzanne is a walking nightmare. She's probably one of the most horrible people I've ever met, and I've met a lot of self-proclaimed sinners.

Maybe that's what triggered what happened next. Maybe even Hell and all its inhabitants are too good for Suzanne Rothschild-Andrews-Stigsson, because whatever lives inside me went straight for her slender throat.

Or at least that's what Coop tells me. I remember vaguely hopping over the back of Knuckles's couch, the one we sat on so many nights, watching TV and eating popcorn, propped up on fluffy pillows.

I remember skin-to-skin contact, my breathing growing ragged, the crack of the beautiful hardwood floor on my knees, and then I don't remember anything else until Coop was on top of my back, prying my fingers from Suzanne's luscious hair.

"Trixie Lavender, let go or I'll be forced to do something drastic!" Coop ordered in my ear, her arm around my neck in a grip of steel.

The second I heard Coop's voice was the second I let my fingers release, shaking them out with wild abandon as though it would ward off the harm I'd surely done.

Livingston flew around the living room, flapping his wings and hooting, sending Suzanne scurrying in a crab-like walk to a corner where, I saw through my red haze of rage, she huddled, shivering violently.

Coop threw me to the floor on my back and straddled my hips, gripping my face so hard I thought my jaw would break and my teeth would crumble in my mouth. "Trixie Lavender! Look at me this instant!"

I fought to focus, every muscle in my body tight, cinching up along my arms and thighs until they quivered. Slowly, her face became clearer as she hauled me up and wrapped her arms around my body, rocking me back and forth until I was coherent enough to ask, "Is she dead?"

Coop inhaled and pressed her cheek to the top of my head. "No. Though, I can see why you wished her so."

Then I remembered why I had such residual anger. Usually after a possession, I'm wiped out, but not this time—not entirely. "Did you hear what she said on the phone?"

Coop continued to rock me back and forth, to and fro, slowly easing the tension in my body. "I heard what *you* said, and it was enough for me to understand your wrath."

My throat was raw and my voice raspy. "Was there screaming?"

"From who? You or her?"

I cringed. "Either-or."

"Then both. You were calling her a wicked-wicked little pig and she was begging for her life and then you squeezed her throat."

I gasped, and it hurt my throat to do so, but I suppose it's nothing less than what I deserve for my outburst. "Did my eyes roll to the back of my head?" Sometimes, that was a side-effect of being a demon.

I felt Coop nod her head. "They did. It's very intimidating. I think Suzanne especially found it intimidating."

Oh, Heaven and the Pearly Gates. "How will we explain?"

"We'll call it a seizure. I've been reading up on some of the behaviors of demonic possession, and some who don't believe it exists dismiss the rage you experience as seizures. I think that will work nicely for the time being. Now breathe, please. Deeply. You're stiff as a corpse."

I don't even want to know why she knows that, but I inhaled deeply. "Do seizures make you try to choke someone?"

"They do if we tell them they do."

Tears sprang to my eyes. "But that's a lie. You're staunchly against lying. I don't want you to lie for me, Coop."

"You lie for me every day, Trixie. Besides, I'm

willing to stretch the truth in favor of being carted off to the place where they examine your head."

"The psych ward," I provided.

"Yes. That's the place. It isn't pleasant from the pictures I've seen, Trixie Lavender. I don't want you to end up in one of those jackets. They're ugly. Alexis Carrington would not approve."

Laughter bubbled up in my throat and spilled out of my dry mouth. "Good point. How do we fix this, Coop?"

She sighed, pulling me closer while rubbing awkward circles on my back. I must remember to mention I like the new perfume she bought. Maybe she'd let me borrow it for my coffee date with Oz.

"You don't fix this, Trixie. I will. You go to the guesthouse and take a shower. You've perspired quite heavily and for lack of a better turn of a phrase, you smell like a New Jersey dump. I'll take care of Suzanne."

That made me fearful. "You won't hurt her?"

"I don't have to. You've already taken care of that today."

I cringed again and leaned back. "Did I hurt her-hurt her, or will she live?"

"She'll need Band-Aids and a therapy session or two."

"But no permanent damage?" I hoped. I prayed.

Coop shook her head, her green eyes intense. "No. Only the lingering mental scars."

I closed my eyes because I couldn't even glance at

Suzanne. "Are you sure you can handle this? You won't let her leave before you're sure she's all right?"

I know Suzanne's the worst, but she doesn't deserve to be beaten to within an inch of her life by a demonically possessed ex-nun.

"I won't, and yes, Trixie. I'm sure I can handle this. Go shower and have a warm cup of tea. I made a kettle just before you tried to kill Suzanne. It should still be warm, and please take Livingston with you—he makes Suzanne Rothschild-Andrews- Stigsson very nervous."

"Coop?"

"Yes, Trixie?"

I popped my eyes open and looked up at her beautiful face, as always a blank canvass. "You're the best friend a girl could have. Thank you."

She wrinkled her nose. "And you smell."

I laughed as she helped me up off Knuckles's living room floor and over to the French doors, calling Livingston, who landed on my shoulder with ease.

As we made our way across the lawn to the guesthouse, I shivered, even as warm as the end of the day was. I hated what I'd done. When Knuckles found out what I'd done, he was going to throttle me.

That made my eyes sting with tears again. I didn't want to lose my friend, but I was all about living in my truth, and truth be told, he might choose to stay with Suzanne no matter what I said.

As I opened our back door to the guesthouse, Livingston said, "Trixie, lass, when you've caught your breath, I have a little nugget to share with ya."

Stepping into the cool interior of the guesthouse, a house I'd come to love and consider myself crazy fortunate to have landed in, I asked, "Is it about Suzanne?"

"Is it ever, dumplin'. Is it ever."

CHAPTER 15

*A*fter a hot shower and a cup of tea, I sat down, laptop in hand, beside Livingston, still sick with shame about what I'd done to Suzanne. Yet, I still found myself absentmindedly gazing at her Facebook page—even as disgusted as I was with her. And let's not forget how disgusted I felt about my behavior, too.

I realize I can't control my behavior when I'm possessed, but it can't be a coincidence that I went for Suzanne's jugular. Though, my demon wasn't exactly selective about who it attacked. Maybe, if I became angry enough, it sensed that and went into fight mode?

I couldn't think about that right now. It was all too much, but sooner or later, I was going to have to literally face my demon.

Sighing, I stroked Livingston's back, finally ready to hear what he'd heard while spending the afternoon with Suzanne.

"So tell me what your little nugget about Suzanne is, pal."

His round, glassy eyes closed and his spine rippled with pleasure. "First, are ya feeling better, lass? That 'twas quite the outburst. One of the louder, more violent ones I've seen, you know."

I looked down at my feet in guilt, fresh tears coming to my eyes. "I'm sorry you had to see that, Livingston."

Leaning forward, he rubbed his round head against my cheek and purred low in his throat. "Oh, lass, ya can't help it. Don't ya tink I know that? Coop knows it, too. You're a good person, Trixie Lavender, ex-nun/tattoo-shop owner. Don't you ever let anyone tell ya otherwise because they'll have to deal wit me, ya hear that? I'll pluck their brains out through their nostrils for speakin' such."

On a sniffle, I chuckled, cupping his sweet face. For all his orneriness, he could be very sweet. "Thank you, Livingston. And yes, I feel better. I just hope Coop can handle Suzanne. Empathy isn't exactly her strong suit, but Suzanne won't be receptive to anything I have to say."

"Never you mind about how Coop handles that wretch. Coop knows what she's doin'. Of that I'm sure."

Taking a deep breath, I smiled at him. "Okay. I'm ready to hear what you have to tell me. Should I gird my loins?"

"I'll let you be the judge. So whilst ya were off playing *The Rockford Files*, she was a busy little bee. Of course, ya already heard what she said to whoever that was on the phone a bit ago, but she's supposed to meet someone at the corner of Wellingham and Burns tonight at nine p.m. to give them sometin'."

I craned my neck to look at him. "To give whom what?"

Livingston shifted position on the arm of the couch, his feet gripping the material. "I don't know, darlin'. She didn't say who it 'twas. She spoke in very short sentences, and I couldn't hear the caller. She kept pacing in and out of the living room, back and forth, prancin' about in that bikini of hers, but I can tell ya this. She was pretty friendly with whoever was on the other end o' that call."

I frowned. "Really?"

"Really. The entire conversation, her hands were flappin' and her mouth was movin'. I didn't hear all of it, but I heard enough to know the superstar was puttin' on a show. You know the one. Where she smiles all coy-like and sticks her body parts out?"

I knew the one. It was the one leaving Knuck mesmerized. As I typed the address Livingston had mentioned into Google maps on my phone, because I fully intended to find out what was there, I asked, "Did she say or do anything else?"

"Hah!" Livingston barked. "She did a whole lot of breathy cooin' like she does when she wants her way. Still couldn't hear much of what she said, but she called the person on the other end o' the line 'daaarling.' Ya know, in that long, drawn out movie star way?"

"Do you remember what time that was?"

"'Round about noon. She doesn't rise much before then. If bein' lazy keeps ya young, she's immortal," he groused.

I smiled. I think it was safe to say we weren't fans of Suzanne here at the Lavender/O'Shea/Livingston household. "And?"

"And then the grievin' widow spent the rest of the day loungin' about as though she were the Queen of Sheba. Never once asked our man Knuckles if he needed anyting after spendin' the entire bloody night with her in the clink. Hasn't bothered to call her friends to see how they're farin' either."

Regret stung my gut like a sharp knife to my intestines. "I should have talked to her before I erupted, Livingston. I missed my chance to ask her why she allowed us to talk to her friends when they see her in such a poor light. I think any opportunity to have a conversation with her is long gone."

Livingston bobbed his head up and down. "After the words you used... Er, your demon used, I don't tink she'll be braidin' your hair at the next sleepover anytime soon, lass. I think the best ting you can do is to leave it alone for now and focus on who offed Agnar, but I'll keep listenin' in if she keeps yappin'."

As I looked at the location Google maps showed me, I realized it was an abandoned building. "It's an abandoned building..." I murmured, more to myself than for Livingston's benefit.

"What is, dumplin'?"

"The address you gave me. So why is Suzanne going to an abandoned building? Meeting another lover, perhaps?"

Livingston sniffed. "I wouldn't put it past her to meet with the devil if he has enough money to bankroll her love of fancy dresses and shoes."

I fought a snort. "That's a fair assessment." Then I sighed from exhaustion. We'd only been looking into this for a couple of days, but it felt like a lifetime since I'd first tripped over poor Agnar. Add in my demonic outburst, and I felt depleted.

"Tell me your troubles, lass."

I couldn't stop thinking about Knuckles, that's what my trouble was. "No trouble, friend," I muttered.

"I can see it all over your face, love. Talk to me."

With a sigh, I closed my eyes and swallowed. "Knuckles is very upset with me for not giving Suzanne enough of a chance at redemption. He seems to have forgotten what she did to him and he's certainly willing to forget she's been sleeping with a close friend of her husband."

Livingston clucked. "You know what that is, don't ya, Trixie? The need to be needed. Knuckles is in a tough spot with missin' his wife as of late. Suzanne needs him, no matter how phony it is. Knuckles needs to be needed. He needs a companion, lass, and he's all mixed up inside over the needin'. You've seen it in his eyes when he thinks no one's lookin'. You've seen how sad he is lately. No one can say what brings that on, I s'pose. It comes and goes, grief does. But that grief clouds your judgment. Makes ya act a fool. But I can promise ya, whatever he said to hurt your feelings, he didn't mean a lick of it. He loves you girls, and Suzanne's going to show her true colors soon enough, and then he'll see. I promise."

I swallowed a fresh batch of tears, the lump in my throat a tight knot. Livingston had real insight, and it wasn't anything I hadn't already thought about, but hearing it out loud made all the difference—it left me feeling validated and a little less sad.

I gave him a watery smile. "Thanks, buddy."

He rubbed his head against my cheek. "Now back to the business o' getting' rid of that tart. Have ya ruled that guttersnipe out as a suspect?"

Had I? "Not entirely, I guess, but while I was showering, it briefly crossed my mind that Suzanne didn't exactly have the opportunity to kill Agnar with a dart laced in this rare deadly toxin. She was riding her bike in the naked bike run. There are witnesses who gave statements backing that up. Not to mention, Agnar was ahead of everyone by about a mile. If she hit him with the dart before he got ahead of them, would it take that long for the toxin to work? I really need to find out what the toxin is. Either way, she might have motive, but I'm not so sure she had the means."

"And the car that hit him? What about that, lass?"

Scratching my hair, I shook my head. "I don't know how in the world that ties into this. She obviously wasn't driving, that's certain. I'm beginning to wonder if the car wasn't just one big coincidence and had nothing to do with trying to kill Agnar at all. Maybe it was just some kid on a joyride. They didn't hurt him, he was only grazed. His bike took most of the impact. What I do know for sure? I'm going to follow her tonight and see who she's meeting. She might not have killed Agnar, but she certainly wants to sink her claws into Knuckles, and I can't let her do that without at least letting him see the whole picture."

"You do realize you could lose his friendship, don't ya, lass?" Livingston warned.

The very thought made me ache all over, especially my heart, which began to thump hard in my chest. "I know, Livingston. But I have to do what's right, and my heart tells me I can't let him go into this blind without having all the facts. What kind of friend would I be if I didn't at least tell him what I heard her say on the phone?"

"If I haven't said it before, I'll say it now, ya have a pure heart, Trixie Lavender. Your soul is kind. Don't let yourself forget that."

Yeah. Look where a kind soul had gotten me. A beat-up aging scream queen and the nicest man I knew steeped in his disappointment for me.

Still, I rubbed Livingston's chin. "I love you, Mr. Cranky Pants. Thanks for giving me some perspective."

"I'm always here. Now about those cookies…?"

I laughed, my head falling back on the couch. "There's always a catch with you, buddy." Sitting back up, I realized I'd somehow hit something on my laptop and enlarged one of Suzanne's pictures on her Instagram page.

Feeling petty, I stuck my tongue out at her—but not before I noticed something I hadn't noticed before.

There were a bunch I didn't have time to look through right now, but one caught my eye. A man, standing in the background on the set of her movie in Brazil. That same man in a different picture, somewhere with Suzanne next to him, surrounded by, guess who? *A bunch of men*. His eyes were adoring as he looked on at Suzanne in one pic, his smile youthful and above all, oddly hopeful.

A man who looked just like Ben Adams...

~

I texted Coop about what I'd just learned and asked her to pinpoint Suzanne's location inside the house. I'd bet my eyeballs Ben was the one Suzanne had an affair with—this grip Lucinda had been talking about.

A quick search of IMDB for the movie *Born in Blood 2* and my mouth fell open. Lucinda had been wrong. Ben wasn't the grip at all—he'd been a cameraman, and I only found that out by clicking on name after name of the crew listed until I got lucky and his picture, along with a list of his work credits, came up.

Sure enough, David Pashman—his real name, as a by the by—had been on the crew of every single movie Suzanne had made over the last three years.

So why the heck was he posing as a journalist from a shoddy tabloid? I needed to find a way to get in touch with him and see what his angle was.

In the meantime, I had an idea. I was pretty good at mimicking voices, even Higgs had said so. If I could get my hands on Suzanne's phone and dial up the list of numbers she'd called today, maybe I could figure out whom she was meeting tonight at an abandoned building.

My phone buzzed, drawing my attention to a text from Coop. *"She's in the shower, and then she said she's going out to clear her head."*

"Is she okay?" I texted, the guilt of my assault on her person still weighing heavy on my heart.

"She's fine, Trixie Lavender. She has some bruises and a cut I tended, but she did accept my explanation about your seizures. It took some doing to talk her out of summoning the police for assault, but she's pretty preoccupied with some meeting, and I was very convincing. So all is well."

"By talk her out of it, do you mean you threatened bodily harm?"

I could almost hear Coop's gasp of outrage from here. *"Most certainly not. I spoke clearly and succinctly and there were no threats involved. I can't blend with humans if I threaten them. Not even Suzanne."*

I laughed. Looks as though I'd dodged another bullet thanks to Coop. *"Find her phone. I'll be right there."*

Dropping a kiss on Livingston's head, I pulled my purse over my shoulder. "Don't eat too many of the cookies, pal. Your tummy won't like you in the morning."

He happily munched on a full plate of Double Stufs while sitting on our small dining room table, getting crumbs all over the white oak wood. "Don't ya worry yourself over me, dumplin'. Go on about your business. I'll see ya later this eve."

I scurried out the back door and made my way toward Knuckles's house, hopping up on his deck to poke my head in the French doors leading to the living room.

"Coop! Where is she?" I whisper-yelled.

Coop sashayed across the living room, Suzanne's phone in hand, her eyes fixed on me. "Still in the shower. She's been in there forever, so you'd better hurry up. What is your plan, Trixie Lavender?"

"I'll tell you later, but I have to hurry!" I turned, almost tripping over one of Knuckles's large planters.

"You'd better slow your stroll, or you won't be hurrying anywhere but to the hospital," she chastised.

"Slow your *roll*," I whispered on a chuckle. "I'll be right back."

I held up a finger to my mouth to quiet her and snuck over the deck, rounding the corner to hide by an enormous rhododendron. Thankfully, Suzanne's phone wasn't password protected, so it was easy to see her most recent calls.

If Livingston was correct, the call came in around twelve this afternoon. As I scrolled her incoming calls,

I realized she'd called Knuckles several times. Where was he, anyway?

The number that called had no name attached, so with fingers crossed, and my heart in my throat, I clicked send and dialed, clearing my throat to gear up to pretend to be Suzanne.

It rang three times, making me think maybe it would go to voice mail, but then, "What's up, Sugar?" a low, growly voice I didn't recognize as any of the people I'd talked to about Suzanne thus far, answered.

On a huge intake of breath, I plowed ahead, my eyes closed, my pulse racing. "Daaarling, I just want to double check the time for our meeting. You did say nine, didn't you?"

I heard some rustling, and then he drawled, "Yep, babe. Can't wait to see you. It's been too long. I miss you."

It was all I could do not to scream in victory. Suzanne had another fish on the line, and I was going to catch her in the act! Then I was going to find out where David Pashman was and why he was pretending to be a journalist from a tabloid.

But then I remembered a piece of advice from Higgs—one lead at a time. So first, the meeting with this unknown man.

Forcing my excitement down to a dull roar, I whispered, "Can't wait, darling. See you then!" and hung up before I dug a hole I couldn't come back from, but I wanted to dance and scream, "I knew it" at the top of my lungs.

I don't know who this man was or where she'd found him on such short notice—her affair with Grady Hanson had only just recently ended, but I was going to prove to Knuckles what a snake she was. I wasn't even going to think about how angry he'd be with me. I could only think about protecting him from this viper.

Now, all I had to do was follow Suzanne to their meeting place, get some video of her deception, and show it to Knuckles. I hated to hurt him, but I had to show him he was wrong about her in the worst possible way.

As I made my way back to the house, Coop stuck her head out the French doors, her gorgeous face in full-on frown. "Give me the phone and stay out of sight. She just got out of the shower."

I lobbed the phone to her like it was a hot potato and ducked back around the house again, heading back to our place with a small measure of relief.

Nine o'clock couldn't come soon enough for me.

CHAPTER 16

I sat in my Caddy—not a terribly inconspicuous vehicle, mind you—in a parking lot across from the meet location, slumped down, waiting for Suzanne to arrive at this abandoned building, which by the by, was a little creepy. It was only five minutes till the hour, but I wanted a head start on this meeting. I wanted to go in prepared in order to catch Suzanne with a smoking gun.

Which isn't to say I was going to confront her. No. No. *No confrontations*. That's not the case at all. I just wanted to catch Suzanne in the act of doing whatever she was going to do with this man somewhere she couldn't see me doing so.

I'd wanted to bring Coop with me, but Goose was the only one at the shop tonight, and Coop had two back-to-back appointments she needed to tend. Besides, this should be easy enough, some quick video from a nicely hidden vantage point, no fuss, no muss, right?

Coop had texted that Suzanne had called for an Uber just before she left for the shop, and that was about a half hour ago. Now all I had to do was wait.

While I waited, I looked at the picture of David Pashman on IMDB, and then I looked him up on Facebook. Could he be the person responsible for killing Agnar? But why? Over Suzanne? Had she somehow talked him into committing murder for her?

If he adored her enough, was obsessed enough, it wasn't so strange, I suppose.

His Facebook page gave me the answer—sort of.

If he hadn't killed Agnar, he'd certainly been obsessed with Suzanne. Her picture was the banner of his Facebook page, along with dozens of stills he'd taken of her on the sets of the various movies he'd done, including the one in Brazil. Maybe he was just a stalker? Far different than a killer, mind you, but regardless, a person of interest.

I think a text to Tansy was in order. What reason could he have had to approach me about Suzanne other than he was obsessed with her?

I shook my head, unclear about his motives beyond his infatuation. Would he kill someone over a woman who'd dumped him, if you listened to Lucinda?

Peering into the darkness, I noted this particular street had little to no available light, and it didn't help that the clouds had moved in and the night was starless. However, that worked to my advantage. Hopefully, I could slip in and out of the car unnoticed.

There wasn't much around either, but I reminded myself, I wasn't going in guns blazing. This was just a quick in and out, nothing more. Still, I shivered at the sight of the building with the windows blown out and the brick facade covered in graffiti.

What a strange place to rendezvous with a man you were probably having an affair with—at least, that's what I assumed this meeting was about—lining up another Sugar Daddy. So why not just meet at a hotel? Maybe that was taking too much of a chance she'd be recognized? Still, the Suzanne I'd learned a little something about probably preferred satin sheets and room service.

My phone buzzed again, a text from Higgs, who I also hadn't told where I was going. He'd been in a particularly rough batch of meetings with doctors and social workers for one of his shelter guys, and I didn't want to put any more stress on him for something as simple as me taking some video while hidden.

"More news from my source at the station..."

You know, I'd sure like to know who the heck his source was and make him or her my new BFF. This way, I could grill the poor person with questions and skip my middleman Higgs altogether. Then maybe he wouldn't feel as though he were betraying the people he once called his own.

"?"

"The toxin found in Agnar's bloodstream is called curare.

It's a plant, apparently. That was what was on the tip of the dart found in his backside."

"You're a peach, Cross Higglesworth! Hope your meetings are going well. Don't forget to eat something!"

"Where are you?"

I made a face at my phone. No way was I telling him what I was doing. He'd be here in two seconds flat, and what he really needed to do was focus on his resident. There was no need for him to be involved because I wasn't getting involved. I was going to stay hidden, get what I needed, and get the heck out.

"Just running some errands. Chat later. Thanks again!"

Now, before you say anything about one more fabrication from this ex-nun, that wasn't a total fabrication. Catching Suzanne in the act of deceiving Knuckles was definitely an errand, right?

I took a peek around again at the deserted street, wondering if I'd missed something or maybe I'd gotten here too late—or maybe the man on the other end of the line had figured me out? Five more minutes and I'd get out and take a peek around. Until then, I typed in the word *curare*.

And then I bit my lower lip. Holy ham and cheese.

The Wiki article said curare was a paralyzing poison, not dangerous if ingested, but used most often by dipping darts into the substance and delivering via blow-dart guns. It was a non-depolarizing muscle relaxant, and only harmful by injection, and can affect respiration…

And get this—it was indigenous to South America.

So, whoa Nellie. As I flipped though all the bits and pieces of conversations I'd had with Suzanne's cohorts, I remembered vaguely Myer saying Agnar had been in the hospital for a severe asthma attack, and Suzanne hadn't batted any eye. Asthma certainly affected your respiration, didn't it?

Ugh! What did this mean? Whatever happened to using a good old-fashioned gun to kill someone?

Frustrated, I was still waiting on Suzanne, I flipped back to David's Facebook page and began really looking at his pictures with a closer eye, but they were mostly of Suzanne and shots from the set, nothing out of the ordinary.

So I went back over to her Instagram. And then I saw it almost all the way at the end of her page. A selfie of her in a bar, judging by the beers lined up behind her, and way in the background was David. I had to enlarge the picture

Guess what David was doing?

Throwing darts.

A cold, black chill slithered up my spine like spider legs, making me grip the cushioned seat of my car. David plus hot for Suzanne plus darts plus shooting a movie in Brazil plus tip of dart found in Agnar's asthma-riddled backside equaled?

A killer!

In the middle of my revelation, Suzanne's Uber pulled up. I knew it was her getting out of the car by the stretch of her long legs as she stepped out and the tinkle of her laughter as she flirted with the driver.

My hands shook as I typed a quick text to Tansy and sent the picture of David Pashman. My breathing grew heavy when I hit send. If my gut hadn't worked before, this time it burned with the knowledge that I knew I was right.

David Pashman had killed Agnar and I'd bet my right arm Suzanne had spoken poorly of her marriage to him, as some often do during pillow talk, and in his obsession, he took it upon himself to rid Suzanne of her problem.

For the life of me, I couldn't figure out how the hit and run fit into this, but maybe it didn't at all. Maybe it really had been just a joy rider, and Agnar getting hit the day he died from a rare toxin was a fluke? Either way, that would have to wait. For now, catching Suzanne in the act was the business of the day.

As Suzanne flitted across the street, graceful as a butterfly floating along a warm breeze, I once more admired how pretty she was. I wouldn't mind the kind of grace she exhibited in heels and a skirt, but I was glad I had sneakers on as I watched her enter the building then slunk out of my car, closing the door as quietly as an old, rusty Caddy would allow.

Phone in hand, I slipped through the shadows, because I'd watched one police show or another where someone said it was best to stay low and in the darkest places when following a human lead, and headed for the entrance to the building.

As I scurried across the crumbling sidewalk, I followed Suzanne's path, entering the building to the damp, musty smell of a place long unloved. The floor was covered in debris, all manner of debris, left in damp piles of rubble.

The clack of her heels had stopped, leaving me to wonder where she'd gone. The building was three stories tall, she could be anywhere in this heap, but it still left me wondering why she chose such a remote, not to mention filthy place to meet her newest lover.

And then I heard her voice, that breathy coo she worked so hard to utilize to her advantage. "Mathew? Where are you, darling?"

I followed the sound into an enormous room with piles of broken pallets and discarded beer bottles. There was only one window, but it let in enough light for me to see outlines of an old mattress, likely from someone in the homeless community.

"Mathew? Where are you? It's filthy in here, darling. I need to see your handsome face so we can get out of here!"

There's the Suzanne I'd come to know and despise, Heaven forgive me. I crouched down behind a stack of pallets and waited, my heart crashing in my chest, my phone at the ready. I didn't know how much actual video I'd get with the poor lighting, but I'd surely get audio.

Out of the shadows, a hulking figure emerged, a large bag in hand. Man, if this was Mathew, he was the size of a freightliner. His shadow loomed over Suzanne by at least a foot, and that's saying something, as Suzanne was at least five-seven or so.

"Darling!" Suzanne cried as he moved toward her. She put her hand in her expensive purse as I clicked the video app on my phone to the on position.

Mathew approached, reaching for her, and that was when Suzanne pulled something from her purse.

I couldn't quite see what it was—you know how that goes in the dark, right? You can pinpoint shapes, but not necessarily connect the image with your brain?

Well, I couldn't see, that is, until I saw.

Know what I saw?

You've likely already guessed.

Yep. If you guessed a big fat menacing-looking gun —you'd win the chicken dinner.

CHAPTER 17

"Stop right there, darling," Suzanne chirped, quite pleasantly, I might add, for someone who was holding a man at gunpoint. She waved the gun at him, the shape of it arcing through the air in her hand.

"Susie?" Mathew called out, his tone clearly confused. "It's me, honey. Put that thing away before you get hurt!"

I could only imagine the look on Suzanne's face as she realized Mathew didn't think she knew who he was. She'd used an over-exaggerated expression of sweet concern at least a hundred times while allowing Knuckles to cater to her every whim.

"I know *exactly* who you are, lover."

"Then what the heck are you doing?" he asked, his tone clearly pained as he took a step forward, only to have Suzanne wave the gun again.

She threw her head back, her long hair nothing

but a silhouette in the dark building, and tinkled a laugh—one of those laughs Coop could take a lesson from, by the way. It was eerily sweet, definitely twisted. "I'm taking care of business of course, darling."

I imagine, at this point, Mathew was stunned, though I couldn't tell from his expression. His face was a dark shadow in the blackness of the building, but his body language did the expressing for him. He stopped dead in his tracks and dropped his bag, his stiff arms going to his sides.

"I don't get it," he fretted. "What are you doing with a gun, Susie? I'd never hurt you, sugar. You know that!"

Suzanne sighed long and wistful. "Oooo, but I'd hurt *you*. You killed my husband, Mathew. I can't just let that stand without some form of punishment, can I?"

Wait—whaaat? This man had shot the lethal dose of curare into Agnar's backend? No. That had to have been David. So what the frack was going on here? Suzanne couldn't be here to defend Agnar's honor after what she'd said about him on the phone? No way I'd believe that. So how did she know this Mathew, anyway? Was he one of her minions like David? Another conquest?

Color me confused and dying to hear what they said next. Even as I thought I wouldn't be able to hear a word of it due to my pulse throbbing in my ears, I stayed crouched with both ears at attention.

"But you *paid* me to kill your husband!" he

defended, his long, muscled arms extending toward Suzanne in pleading fashion.

She chuckled and took a step closer to Mathew. "Well, I *was* going to pay you to kill that cheap SOB. Ten grand was the deal, right? But you didn't do the job, darling, did you?"

Holy Hannah, Mathew was the one who'd been driving the Crown Vic... Suzanne had paid him to kill Agnar.

"You know I tried, Suzanne! Do you have any idea how hard it was to get past the cops with that car? I hit him, Susie! I know I did!"

I closed my eyes and swallowed hard. Aw, man, what had I gotten myself into? This was supposed to be easy, for Pete's sake! *In and out, remember, Trixie? No confrontation.* How was I going to get the heck out of this? In order to get out of the building, I had to go past them.

Suzanne straightened her arm, her stance wide. "Do you have any idea how stupid you are? You didn't kill him, you blundering idiot! Some rare toxic substance did!"

Mathew's hands clenched into balled fists—fists I'd hate for him to use on me. "What difference does it make? He's dead. Isn't that what you wanted? You said once he was dead, we'd be together!"

"I said I'd pay you for a service," she replied coolly. "That service was not rendered, Mathew."

Now Mathew's body went rigid, like a tall Redwood, as the picture obviously became clear. "You stupid, selfish little b—"

"Uh-uh-uh!" Suzanne chastised a warning as though she were speaking to a small child, pointing the gun directly at his chest. "No name calling. Is that any way to talk to your lover—a woman you professed to love until your dying day?"

So Mathew had messed up, but *David* was the one who'd done it right.

None of that mattered now. All that mattered was another murder was about to occur—Mathew's.

Holy cats and dogs. My mouth went dry and my now crouch-achy legs almost gave out. Yet, I was immobilized by this conversation, mesmerized by what was playing out right before my eyes.

"Don't move, Suzanne!" a voice shouted from the deep black pit that was the doorway.

Oh, thank the stars, maybe help had arrived? As my head swiveled, and I heard the rush of a pair of feet, I squinted into the darkness and my stomach clenched into a tight knot. On the contrary, help hadn't arrived at all.

"David?" I heard Suzanne whisper in disbelief, taking a step back as *he* pointed a gun at *her*.

I fought a loud gasp, stuffing my fist into my mouth to keep from squealing my dismay like a pig. David had obviously come to confront Suzanne, and he had a gun to make her listen.

Heaven and a pepperoni pizza, now we didn't have one gun in the mix but two—not to mention, two mad-as-a-hatter murderers ready to pull the triggers.

The game was certainly afoot.

"David, darling, what are you doing here?"

I couldn't help but hear the genuine surprise in her voice, the shock, and I had to wonder—what the heck was going on?

David rushed forward, holding the gun up and pointing it at Suzanne's head. "Don't you *darling* me! I did this for you, and this is how you betray me?" he screamed, jarring me to the core.

Somewhere along the way, the clouds had shifted and the moon appeared, sending a shaft of light into the one window of the building. I could clearly see David's face, the pain written all over his smooth, youthful features.

And I also saw Suzanne narrow her gaze in his direction. "What are you talking about, you fool?" she bellowed, stomping her foot.

David's lower lip trembled, his words sounding like they were fighting their way out of his throat. "You said you loved me!" he cried. "You told me your husband was horrible, that he was going to leave you penniless, with nothing—that he hurt you! You said being with him was torture. You said if you could get away from him, you'd be with me, but it was impossible. You said he'd find you and make you come back! You said he'd leave you with nothing! So I killed him! I killed him for hurting you! And all this time you were cheating on me with *him?*"

Now Suzanne's eyes popped open wide in surprise, but the three-way standoff continued. No one backed down, no one moved. "Loved you?" She laughed a cruel chuckle. "I never loved you, you moron, but thanks for taking care of business, because *this* idiot sure didn't. Now give me the gun, David."

"*Nooo!*" He screamed so loud, the entire building shook with the sound of his voice, making me cringe while he closed in on Suzanne. His pain was crystal clear, and the empty promises she'd made had torn him up enough to make him kill for her. "You said we would be together, Suzanne! You said it over and over, but you lied! You liiied!"

Okay, so here's the thing, I was so wrapped up in the dialogue between these three people, so entranced by the dynamic that had been revealed, I sort of forgot everything else. Like, doing the smart thing while I was hidden.

Which would have been to text Higgs and Tansy while they were screaming at each other and my legs still had a chance at un-kinking themselves, yes?

But nooo. I'd been so lost in this drama, so determined to videotape Suzanne's deception, I forgot all about the smart thing to do—the right thing to do long past the time I should have done it.

And admittedly, I remembered too late because my aching legs, legs that kept me hidden securely behind the stack of pallets, gave out just as I pressed send to share with Higgs and Tansy the address of the building and what was happening right before my very eyes.

So yes. Then my legs collapsed, and what happened next? I fell out from behind the pallets and rolled into the outer corner of the room.

In the exact spot the light from that once-hidden-behind-the-clouds moon shone on the floor. Just lucky, I guess.

As three very surprised faces looked down at me, I gave them a weak smile based on a cringe. "So, heeey, guys. Funny story. Three murderers and an ex-nun walk into an abandoned building…"

CHAPTER 18

$\mathcal{R}$emember when I said there were two guns in the mix? Indeed, that was the truth, and now they were both pointed at me.

Suzanne looked down at me, her face a mask of twisted fury, while David's eyes were wild and unblinking as his hand quivered. Mathew stood between the two, rooted to the spot instead of running for his life.

Me? Well, my throat was drier than the Mojave and my legs trembled like Jell-O as I lie on the dirty ground, the stench of mold and empty beer bottles in my nostrils.

"Get up!" Suzanne screamed at me, stomping her foot on the ground. "Get up, you interfering, blathering, dowdy imbecile!"

You know, I don't want to take exception here, but dowdy is rather mean. I'm not dowdy. I'm average, thank you. But I suppose she wouldn't want to haggle about that right now. So I rose to my feet, but not without struggle, because listen, I could stand to do a sit-up or two to strengthen my core.

Note to self, if the universe sees fit to allow you your life, Trixe "Lazy" Lavender, buy a treadmill pronto.

As I stood, both guns swung in different directions, seemingly with no particular place to go. I mean, who was shooting whom here, right?

Instantly, my hands flew up in the air. I can't say for sure what happened to my phone, but for all the good it would do me now, I think I dropped it when my legs gave out, but I prayed my texts to Tansy and Higgs had gone through.

So now, let me lay this out for you. Suzanne had a gun. David had a gun. Mathew and little ole' me were at a disadvantage. It stood to reason, if the people without guns made a move, one of them was going to get shot.

We were in such close proximity in this bizarre standoff, it would be impossible to make a break for it, and both of us knew it. So here we were, two of us afraid to make a move, and two gun happy, lunatics.

"Miss Lavender?" David squeaked, sweat glistening above his lip and leaving a fine sheen along his forehead. "What are *you* doing here?"

I licked my lips and swallowed hard, wiping my clammy hands on my thighs. "You know, funny you should ask. I was going to ask you the same thing—*Ben.*"

"Ben?" Suzanne squawked, her eyes glittering in the dark. "Who's Ben?"

Ah. My opportunity to stall. Every killer has a story, according to my pal Stevie, and they all want to share theirs. This was my chance to figure out how to get out of this bind. "Ben's a journalist for *Truth Seeker Confidential*," I replied, hoping my voice didn't wobble as much as my legs. "He asked me a bunch of questions about you just yesterday, didn't you, Ben? But you didn't tell me you knew her personally. How do you know each other, Ben?"

"Oh, please! *He's not a journalist*!" Susanne spat, her lips thinning. "He's a lowly cameraman who worked on the crew of some of my movies—and his name isn't Ben, it's David, but you already know that, don't you?"

David smiled at both of us, his lips lifting in a macabre grin. "What can I say? I lied," he said with a shrug of his shoulders. "She's right. My name really is David. I just wanted to know if you knew where she was. I saw you with her the night I killed her husband, and then I found out you owned the tattoo store, got your name, and followed you to your big, scary ex-cop friend's apartment. So I took a shot in the dark and asked you some questions, and it paid off. After that, finding Suzanne was easy. Then I followed her here tonight."

I pretended to be shocked he'd duped me, even though I already knew. "And you followed her here tonight to what, Ben? Why are you here? What do you want?"

His face went from pleased with himself to irate in two seconds flat as he rocked back and forth on unsteady feet. "I was going to find out why she wouldn't answer my calls…but now I'm going to kill her, of course. She lied to me, Miss Lavender!" he reasoned. "She promised me we'd be together then refused to take my calls! I thought it was because her husband was keeping her from me. I thought she couldn't get to me because of *him*, so I eliminated the problem!"

"I can't believe you killed Agnar!" Suzanne shrieked as though David had inconvenienced her by giving her exactly what she'd wanted to begin with—Agnar dead. What difference did it make to her who'd done the deed?

But I ignored her and my clammy hands and racing heart. "By shooting him with a dart laced in curare, right, David?" I asked, taking a small step back.

I don't know why I did that, it just made sense to put space between us. Everything was closing in on me, overwhelming me.

Suzanne gasped, her mouth falling open. "How do you know that?"

"Well," I drawled, trying with every ounce of restraint I had not to let her know how terrified I was. "You'd know that, too, if you gave a fig! Higgs told me just a little bit ago they figured out the substance used to kill Agnar was curare—a poisonous plant found in Brazil. You know, where you filmed *Born in Blood 2*?"

"Hah! See, Suzanne?" David yelped in desperation.

"I *do* love you—more than anything! Way more than whoever this is! I'd do anything for you! I killed him. I researched forever, and I would have killed him in Brazil, but he left before I could figure out how to use it—so I brought some back with me, and it was all easier than you think."

I'm not sure I want to know how he got past customs or whatever with that plant, but he sure appeared pretty pleased with himself.

"*You* killed him with a *dart!*" Suzanne ground out, and I wasn't sure if she was impressed or disgusted.

He grinned, boyish and evil as he held the gun up. "I shot that dart laced in curare from at least a hundred yards away. Totally nailed him!"

Suzanne's eyes went wide and for the first time, I saw her hands tremble. "You're insane…" she murmured.

He quivered, his eyes searching her face. "Insane? What's *insane* is thinking I'd let you get hurt. How could you think I'd let you go back to that tyrant? I love you. I trusted you!"

"Join the club, kid," Mathew muttered, his eyes capturing mine in desperation, but I instantly looked away.

Oh, no sir. There'd be no hostage sympathy from me, pal. He may not have done the deed, but he tried. In my book, that made him a killer, too.

Now Suzanne wavered, her eyes flashing her anger. "How could you think I'd ever run away with *you*? You disgust me! You were nothing more than something to amuse me—to occupy me during the boredom of that dreadful shoot!" she said cruelly, crushing David, whose face crumpled right before my eyes.

So here's what I was up against. Three killers: one poor, misguided child, blinded by puppy love; one middle-aged man (I think), blinded by lust and greed; and one rabid nut of a woman who aged like a vampire and had used her body and charms to seduce men into killing her husband.

To say the odds were stacked against me was an underestimation of my snafu. What to do? I could only stall so long. If Tansy and company didn't get here soon, I was a goner, for sure.

Still, there was one little fact nagging at me, and if I was going to leave this place in a body bag, what did I have to lose by asking?

"But why did you ask me to help you find who'd killed Agnar, Suzanne, knowing what you knew? *Why* would you do that?"

She rolled her eyes at me and huffed. "Because I had to throw the scent off *me*, you fool! The first person they suspect is the spouse. Would the woman who tried to have her husband killed actually ask someone to *help* her find his killer? It was hiding in plain sight, of course! I mean, I'm an actress, for heaven's sake. If anyone could pull that off, it was *me*. So I did a little improv."

Except, I never totally fell for it. I'd been suspicious all along, but kudos to her for being so brazen. Though, I don't suppose I should share that with her while she had a gun pointing at my face, but I was impressed by the size of her ego and her faith in her acting skills.

I raised a finger, blindly jumping into this cesspool of murder folk with both feet, and said, "So in summary, Suzanne paid Mathew to kill Agnar. Mathew tried to kill Agnar with his car and failed. David, a.k.a. Ben, succeeded with a dart laced in a substance that's poisonous. Do I have that right so far?" I didn't wait for an answer. "Now what we have is a dilemma. I know a secret I shouldn't, and the rest of you are guilty of committing, at the very least, a class one felony. Where do we go from here?"

"You die!" Suzanne yelled, as she backed away from us and aimed the gun in my direction. "You have to die! You're nothing but a nuisance, hovering over Donald all the time!"

"But wait!" I yelled into the cavernous interior of the room, holding up my hands as my pulse pounded in my ears. "Let's look at the odds here, Suzanne. What if David's a faster draw than you, and he takes you out first? He did hit Agnar in the rear end from a hundred yards while he was on a bike. That's a pretty good shot. Then what? Or what if Mathew, who's the size of an oak tree, overpowers you, gets the gun from you and kills *you* instead?"

Everyone stopped doing anything at that point, making me wonder if these two meatheads could get a clue. I'd basically handed them a shot at getting away, and no one bit. No. They just stood there like we were playing a game of freeze tag.

Suzanne was the first to speak, her eyes cunning and full of hatred. "They won't hurt me, Tipsy. Because they love me—"

And that was when Mathew took his shot. While Suzanne was in the process of gushing over their admiration, he steamrolled her, catching her on her side and knocking her to the ground with a grunt.

She screamed her outrage, the sound ringing in my ears.

It happened so quickly, I reacted on what I have to guess is instinct. I dropped to the ground and flattened myself, trying to crawl to the other side of the room on my belly. But in the pool of light, I saw Suzanne still had the gun, and man, I bet she works out, because she held on to that gun like she was hanging on to her youth.

Kneeing Mathew in a very private place with all her might, she managed to make him scream in pain as he fell off her and she rolled away. Then she held that gun up and pointed it at a surprised David, who'd suddenly become frozen in place while he watched the ensuing chaos.

She fired off a shot, hitting him square in the kneecap, making him howl in agony as he crumbled to the ground, dropping his gun.

When she realized I was making my getaway, she came after me while David screamed in agony on the floor, firing off a shot I, there but for the grace of the universe, managed to escape.

Just as I was about to seek solace behind the pallets,

she fired off another shot and I tripped over my two left feet—one still remembering the sting of being shot. That was when Suzanne dropped her gun, and I thought for sure I could get away. But she came up behind me, grabbing me by the back of my T-shirt. I heard the rip, felt the tug of material against my flesh, and immediately rolled over only to find she'd managed to get her sticky fingers back on the weapon.

In the tussle, I happened to get a peek at where David's gun had landed, and if I could somehow buck her off me, if I could push her far enough away, maybe I had a chance at grabbing it...but it was a really long shot.

Her hair was wild, her expression filled with fury as she looked down at me, her shaky hands wrapped around the gun. Pointing it at my head, her lips thinned as she jammed her beautiful face in mine. "You animal! You tried to *kill* me today!" she hissed, making me cringe at her rage.

"*Suzanne, no!*" someone yelled from somewhere that sounded very far away, distracting her—and that was when I took my shot.

As her head turned, I knocked her arm up and out of the way, sending the gun flying, and then, using the heel of my hand, I gave her an uppercut to the chin, using all my might.

When she fell backward, I sat up, only this time I didn't struggle. No. In fact, I rolled forward and got on my knees, grabbing hold of her shapely leg.

But Suzanne was far craftier and probably in better

shape than I'll ever be, and with one impressive lift of her hips (I'm voting Pilates, but it's painfully obvious I know nothing about exercise), she wrapped both her legs around my neck and began to squeeze until I almost couldn't breathe.

In a panic, unable to get air, scratching at her legs to no avail, I began to feel around for the gun she'd lost. But instead, my fingers found a discarded glass bottle. With my heart crashing against my ribs, I did the only thing I could do.

I lifted my arm high, smashed the bottle on the ground, felt the crunch of glass then rammed the jagged edge into her leg and twisted with all the energy I had left in me.

Suzanne's howl of pain rang in my ears as she let go of my neck.

I pushed myself back up on my knees, my breaths coming sharp and painful, my chest heaving as I gasped for air.

And just as I was about to ensure Suzanne was down for the count, Higgs was there, hauling me upward, pulling me away.

"Tansy!" he shouted. "Over here!"

Then Tansy and Oz were there with a bunch of police officers swarming the building as I let Higgs help me to the corner of the room. Flashlights swirled around, footsteps pounded while Suzanne's high-pitched screams for mercy rang out. Oz gathered up David, who howled in agony, too, and some other officers hauled Mathew up and helped him hobble off.

I heard Mathew scream, "I chickened out—I swear! I didn't hit him! I didn't hit him!"

I fell against Higgs in relief, letting my forehead rest on his chest, forcing the air back into my lungs, sweat dripping from my hair.

"Trixie?" he said, his voice chock full of concern as he cupped my cheeks in his hands. "Are you okay? Holy cow, what happened? I got your text and flew over here as fast as I could!"

"I came to prove Suzanne was a horrible person. I swear on my morning coffee for the rest of my life, I didn't intend to get involved. The plan was to hide while I videotaped her meeting. I had no idea Suzanne hired a hit man and that was who she was meeting. I thought she was meeting the next guy she was going to bilk for some cash, not a murderer. I told you she was a horrible person," I said on a ragged breath.

Higgs laughed, pulling me into his arms to give me a hug—a hug that left me feeling secure, safe. "I'm guessing you're going to tell me all about how right you were?"

When I pulled away, suddenly unsure about these strange feelings I was having for Higgs in the middle of such a crisis, I poked a finger into his hard chest. "Oh, you bet I am, buster. Man, am I ever."

"You know, you have to stop scaring the life out of me, Sister Trixie. You'll give me a heart attack before I'm forty this way."

"Oh, no. That's not going to have anything to do with me, Higglesworth. That award goes to all the cheeseburgers you eat. You do know red meat is bad for you, right?"

"How can a cheeseburger be so wrong when it tastes so right?" he teased, brushing my hair from my face with his fingers.

Suddenly, I was depleted. My bones felt like butter and my eyes were grainy. "I think I'd like to go home now, Higgs. I promise I'll explain everything when we get there, okay?"

"You got it, Sister Trixie. While we're going over why you came to an abandoned building this late, all alone, with no backup, let's discuss those rules we never went over, okay? Rule number one: Do not chase after a suspect in a murder investigation *alone*. Call Higgs so he can talk you out of such nonsense."

I sighed and let Higgs wrap his arm around my shoulder as he helped me through the throng of people. "Rules, shmules. I swear on Angela Lansbury, I already told you, I wasn't doing anything dangerous."

"Really, Nancy Drew? How do not one, but *two* guns and three bad guys constitute not doing anything dangerous?"

"Oh, peeshaw. That's nothing. You should have seen the time Sister Francis Marie and I went to the penitentiary in Salem to meet Big Wallace Farber…"

Higgs's laughter echoed on our way out the door and into the cool night air.

And once more, I found myself grateful for these new people in my life.

So very grateful.

~

*A*fter Tansy and her detectives finished questioning me and left our house, I sat out on the deck with Higgs, who waited with me so we could talk to Knuckles about what had happened tonight. My heart ached for what he'd hear, and I hated that I was going to be the one to tell him about Suzanne's awfulness again.

He'd been out of touch all day long, and I was beginning to think maybe he'd gone somewhere out of town, until I heard the rumble of his bike in the driveway. Higgs had sent him a text when he couldn't reach him by phone.

I guess he got the message, and now I had to face him after he'd been so upset with me and tell him his one-time love was a murderer—or had *hired* a murderer.

"Trixie!" he called, running up the stairs to scoop me up in a tight hug. "Gravy, girl. Are you okay?"

Higgs slapped him on the back. "Question is, are you?"

Knuckles nodded his head, his eyes full of pain. "I'm okay, you mind if I have a minute alone with our girl?"

"I don't mind at all," Higgs said softly. "I'm going to head out. Call me if you need me." He gave us both a smile and a wave, likely knowing everything was going to be all right between us, and left.

I squeezed Knuckles back hard before I asked, "Like Higgs said, the question is, are you okay?"

He set me away from him but I saw his eyes—and they held shame. I hated that. "I'm fine, Trixie girl. Just fine."

I knew Knuckles was embarrassed. I knew his pride was aching from the sting of Suzanne's behavior, but that was unacceptable to me. He was kind and gentle and no way would I let him gloss this over. I wanted him to know how special he was, and that his longing for Candice was no reason to accept the kind of cruelty Suzanne had doled out.

I pulled him to the edge of the deck where we'd spent many nights, staring up at the stars while we let our legs dangle over the edge, and sat down, taking him with me.

"I don't believe you. Talk to me, friend," I said, tucking my arm into his and resting my head on his broad shoulder.

"Me? Don't you worry about me, little lady. It's *you* I'm worried about. She could have killed you, and I'd have never forgiven myself. I'm sure sorry I didn't listen to you and Goose."

I shook my head, tears stinging my eyes. "Forget it. Long since a faded memory. But please, talk to me about how you feel about this. *Please.*"

He looked up into the sky. "Nothin' for you to concern yourself with, kiddo. I'm a big boy. I can take a hit with the best of 'em."

"Suzanne hurt you, that makes me concerned. I don't like to see my friends hurt."

"*I'm* not hurt so much as my ego, I s'pose. I was a

dang fool to believe her—again. I really wanted to believe she'd changed, Trixie. I fell for it like the old fool I am. Hook, line and sinker. Nothin's been right since Candice has gone. I think single's the way to go from here on out. Best part about my life is you girls and the shop these days. I'll be fine. Don't you worry."

My heart clenched and tightened in my chest. "Oh, I'm not worried about you, mister. You're awesomeness times a fajillion. You know what I'm worried about? I'm worried someone as awful as Suzanne has jaded you, that because Candice was one in a million, you think you'll never be able to find another like her. But don't you see, you shouldn't think that. Candice was...well, *Candice*. Her memory should be treasured, honored—always. How can you ever forget the woman who so adored you? She was a wonderful, loving, amazing part of your life, and she always will be. But I'd like you to consider something, if you would."

"What's that, Trixie?"

I squeezed his arm and gripped his beefy hand. "Consider that maybe there are two in a million. That maybe there's someone else out there who's just as special in her own unique way, and when the two of you collide, the world will implode from so much awesome in one stinkin' couple."

Knuckles, my dear, kind, sweet friend, let out a breath that shuddered ever so slightly. I know he hated to appear vulnerable. I know his longing for Candice outweighed his need to show everyone that vulnerability because in his day, being a man meant showing no weakness.

Yet, it was this very vulnerability, seeping through his cracks, that made him the kind of man I'd come to look up to—a man with a heart he might not like wearing on his sleeve, but he wore it there anyway.

"I knew Suzanne was a bad egg, kiddo. Believe me, I did…deep down, anyway. But she needed me. Sometimes, that takes away some of the loneliness—when you're needed."

A tear stung my eyes and I had to gulp back the urge to let them flow freely. "She needed you for all the wrong reasons, and I know you know that in your heart of hearts. But *we* need you, too, Knuckles—me, and Coop, and even Mr. Cranky Pants. *We need you.* We need you to be happy and healthy and with a wonderful woman who treats you like the absolute gem of a prince you are."

I gave his shoulder a nudge with mine. "Now, listen. I know this sounds like a bunch of bunk coming from a friend, and you'll probably think I'm only saying this because I *am* your friend, but you mean the world to us. You *are* our world—a huge part of it—one of the reasons we have a shop, and a place to live, and the feeling that we belong. That we matter. I know it's not the same as having a life partner, but we're here, Knuck. We'll *always* be here for you. Promise."

He wrapped his big arm around my shoulders and pulled me in close, his voice gruff. "I like you, Trixie girl. I like you so-so much," he said, mimicking Coop's favorite phrase.

My heart swelled and my eyes filled with tears of so much gratitude, I almost burst. "I like you, too, Knuckles. *So-so much.*"

EPILOGUE

Three days later...

Myer Blackmoore held up his arm and smiled wide from his seat in Coop's tat chair. "This is absolutely fantastic, Coop. Thank you! From the bottom of my heart, thank you."

Coop nodded, her eyes intense as she pulled off her gloves and patted Myer on the back with an awkward thump. "My pleasure, Myer Blackmoore. Wear it in good health."

Myer was too enthralled with his new tattoo to notice the strange way Coop addressed him, and he *should* be enthralled. It was a beautiful tribute to his friend—a tattoo of a man on a bicycle with Agnar's name and the dates of his birth and his death.

The group—minus Grady Hanson, who'd left in an embarrassed hurry—was finally on their way back to LA after being cleared by the police, and they were happy to be doing so. So many bad things had happened to them since their arrival—the death of their friend, the downfall of Suzanne—it was time for them all to move forward. But they'd stopped in to commemorate their last ride with their friend by getting tattoos.

Seeing the shop full like this brought so much joy to my heart as I watched everyone mingling—even Knuckles, who chatted with Myer despite his heartache over Suzanne. Though quiet these last couple of days, with all the news reports on Suzanne and David, Knuckles appeared lighter of heart, and I hoped he'd heed my words of the other night.

Because I'd meant them from the depths of my soul.

Jeff still couldn't remember anything about this message he claimed to have for me. Thus, the search continued to find a way to help him remember. As frustrating as that was, I had to remind myself patience was a virtue and let it go for the time being. That we were all happy, safe, and together meant everything to me. The rest could wait.

My demon, still nameless, hadn't reappeared since I'd knocked Suzanne around, but I wasn't in a rush to find out what its name was, either. I know the day will come when I have to hit that problem head-on, but right now, with the shop just picking up steam, I set it aside in favor of the hope this demon would go away and never come back.

Edwin sidled up to the front counter and leaned in, his tattoo from Goose—a sculpture he'd asked me to sketch, one Agnar had treasured—freshly covered with cling wrap.

"I don't suppose you'd put in a good word for me with your friend Coop, would you?"

I looked into his handsome face and shook my head in the negative. "No, sir. I absolutely would not." Then I laughed to soften the blow. Edwin knew he was a cad, and he also knew I didn't want one of my dearest friends involved with a cad.

He tipped his head and smiled. "Fair enough. Hey, I was looking over your Facebook page…you know, you being an ex-nun gone tattoo shop owner…and I happened to see a picture of you with a rare artifact. Mind telling me where you found it?"

I gave him a confused look. A rare artifact? Did he mean Sister Gwendolyn Ann? She was indeed pretty old, and rarely did one live as long as she. "I don't know what you mean. Can you pull it up on your phone?"

He dragged his phone from the breast pocket of his jacket and scrolled until he found what he was looking for. "This one here. See that statue? That's pretty old. Can't remember where I saw it, but I do remember someone mentioning it's been around for thousands of years. Has some sort of alleged curse attached to it, I think. Know anything about it?"

I forced my face to remain impassive, but my heart chugged and lurched in my chest.

It was a picture of me with the relic that had started this whole possession mess. I'd totally forgotten about putting it on my Facebook page. It was the only one I had of me from my days as a nun.

Licking my suddenly dry lips, I fought to keep the shakiness from my voice. Edwin knew about rare art. Maybe he could help? Maybe he could make sense of this?

"You know, I don't know anything about it, other than it was in the convent the entire time I was there. But if you ever find out any details, I'd really appreciate knowing its history?"

He reached over the countertop and pinched my cheek with a smile. "You bet, sunshine. I've got your email." Then he turned to face his friends. "Can we please leave this state now? I need some palm trees and a good stiff drink, folks."

Everyone laughed as they gathered their bags and headed toward the door, shaking hands and smiling. Lucinda gave me a quick hug and whispered, "Remember what I said, Trixie. If you ever want some help with your personal style, I'm your girl. Now I'm *really* your girl after what you did for Agnar."

I smiled at her and nodded my head. "I'll keep that in mind."

As they all plowed out, yet another chapter in this new life closing, Higgs passed them on his way in, pizza boxes in hand.

"Lunch has officially arrived, folks. Get it while it's hot and gooey!"

With a sigh of relief, I followed everyone to the back of the store where we had a table and enough chairs for all of us to share a meal, lovingly stroking Livingston's head on my way. We all took our usual places, except for Coop, who'd stopped to answer the shop's phone.

"Higgs, did you remember to get black olives?" I asked as he pulled in his chair and reached for a pizza box.

"Would I forget something as important as that?" he asked with a chuckle. "The last time I forgot, you said, 'the next pizza I brought into this store better have black olives or you die an ugly death, Cross Higglesworth!'"

I pointed a finger at him and wagged it under his nose. "And I meant it, buddy. What is this pineapple and ham nonsense anyway?"

"Trixe Lavender?" Coop called, holding up the shop's phone. "Phone call."

I turned to Higgs and gave him my best sour nun face. "I'd better not come back and find pineapple on my pizza, buddy."

We all chuckled as I made my way to the phone, taking it from Coop, who went off to eat. "Hello, this is Trixie Lavender."

"Trixie?"

My stomach sank right to my feet.

I knew this voice. I knew it, and had once cherished it. It was the voice that had betrayed me not so long ago.

"Yes?" I said, though my voice trembled something fierce.

"This is Father O'Leary from Saint Aloysius By The Sea...

The End

Thank you so much for joining me for book 2 in the Nun of Your Business Mysteries! I so hope you'll come back for book 3, titled *House of The Rising Nun*, coming soon!

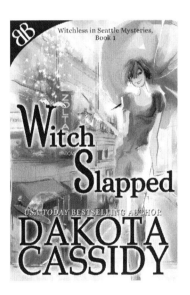

Chapter 1

"Left, Stevie! Left!" my familiar, Belfry, bellowed, flapping his teeny bat wings in a rhythmic whir against the lash of wind and rain. "No, your other left! If you don't get this right sometime soon, we're gonna end up resurrecting the entire population of hell!"

I repositioned him in the air, moving my hand to the left, my fingers and arms aching as the icy rains of Seattle in February battered my face and my last clean outfit. "Are you sure it was *here* that the voice led you? Like right in this spot? Why would a ghost choose a cliff on a hill in the middle of Ebenezer Falls as a place to strike up a conversation?"

"Stevie Cartwright, in your former witch life, did the ghosts you once spent more time with than the living always choose convenient locales to do their talking? As I recall, that loose screw Ferdinand Santos decided to make an appearance at the gynecologist. Remember? It was all stirrups and forceps and gabbing about you going to his wife to tell her where he hid the toenail clippers. That's only one example. Shall I list more?"

Sometimes, in my former life as a witch, those who'd gone to the Great Beyond contacted me to help them settle up a score, or reveal information they took to the grave but felt guilty about taking. Some scores and guilty consciences were worthier than others.

"Fine. Let's forget about convenience and settle for getting the job done because it's forty degrees and dropping, you're going to catch your death, and I can't spend all day on a rainy cliff just because you're sure someone is trying to contact me using *you* as my conduit. You aren't like rabbit ears on a TV, buddy. And let's not forget the fact that we're unemployed, if you'll recall. We need a job, Belfry. We need big, big job before my savings turns to ashes and joins the pile that was once known as my life."

"Higher!" he demanded. Then he asked, "Speaking of ashes, on a scale of one to ten, how much do you hate Baba Yaga today? You know, now that we're a month into this witchless gig?"

Losing my witch powers was a sore subject I tried in quiet desperation to keep on the inside.

I puffed an icy breath from my lips, creating a spray from the rain splashing into my mouth. "I don't hate Baba," I replied easily.

Almost too easily.

The answer had become second nature. I responded the same way every time anyone asked when referring to the witch community's fearless, ageless leader, Baba Yaga, who'd shunned me right out of my former life in Paris, Texas, and back to my roots in a suburb of Seattle.

I won't lie. That had been the single most painful moment of my life. I didn't think anything could top being left at the altar by Warren the Wayward Warlock. Forget losing a fiancé. I had the witch literally slapped right out of me. I lost my entire being. Everything I've ever known.

Belfry made his wings flap harder and tipped his head to the right, pushing his tiny skull into the wind. "But you no likey. Baba booted you out of Paris, Stevie. Shunned you like you'd never even existed."

Paris was the place to be for a witch if living out loud was your thing. There was no hiding your magic, no fear of a human uprising or being burned at the stake out of paranoia. Everyone in the small town of Paris was paranormal, though primarily it was made up of my own kind.

Some witches are just as happy living where humans are the majority of the population. They don't mind keeping their powers a secret, but I came to love carrying around my wand in my back pocket just as naturally as I'd carry my lipstick in my purse.

I really loved the freedom to practice white magic anywhere I wanted within the confines of Paris and its rules, even if I didn't love feeling like I lived two feet from the fiery jaws of Satan.

But Belfry had taken my ousting from the witch community much harder than me—or maybe I should say he's more vocal about it than me.

So I had to ask. "Do you keep bringing up my universal shunning to poke at me, because you get a kick out of seeing my eyes at their puffiest after a good, hard cry? Or do you ask to test the waters because there's some witch event Baba's hosting that you want to go to with all your little familiar friends and you know the subject is a sore one for me this early in the 'Stevie isn't a witch anymore' game?"

Belfry's small body trembled. "You hurt my soul, Cruel One. I would never tease about something so delicate. It's neither. As your familiar, it's my job to know where your emotions rank. I can't read you like I used to because—"

"Because I'm not on the same wavelength as you. Our connection is weak and my witchy aura is fading. Yadda, yadda, yadda. I get it. Listen, Bel, I don't hate BY. She's a good leader. On the other hand, I'm not inviting her over for girls' night and braiding her hair either. She did what she had to in accordance with the white witch way. I also get that. She's the head witch in charge and it's her duty to protect the community."

"Protect-schmotect. She was over you like a champion hurdler. In a half second flat."

Belfry was bitter-schmitter.

"Things have been dicey in Paris as of late, with a lot of change going on. You know that as well as I do. I just happened to be unlucky enough to be the proverbial straw to break Baba's camel back. She made me the example to show everyone how she protects us...er, *them*. So could we not talk about her or my defunct powers or my old life anymore? Because if we don't look to the future and get me employed, we're going to have to make curtains out of your tiny wings to cover the window of our box under the bridge."

"Wait! There he is! Hold steady, Stevie!" he yelled into the wind.

We were out on this cliff in the town I'd grown up in because Belfry claimed someone from the afterlife— someone British—was trying to contact me, and as he followed the voice, it was clearest here. In the freezing rain...

Also in my former life, from time to time, I'd helped those who'd passed on solve a mystery. Now that I was unavailable for comment, they tried reaching me via Belfry.

The connection was always hazy and muddled, it came and went, broken and spotty, but Belfry wasn't ready to let go of our former life. So more often than not, over the last month since I'd been booted from the community, as the afterlife grew anxious about my vacancy, the dearly departed sought any means to connect with me.

Belfry was the most recent "any means."

"Madam *Who*?" Belfry squeaked in his munchkin voice, startling me. "Listen up, matey, when you contact a medium, you gotta turn up the volume!"

"Belfryyy!" I yelled when a strong wind picked up, lashing at my face and making my eyes tear. "This is moving toward ridiculous. Just tell whoever it is that I can't come to the phone right now due to poverty!"

He shrugged me off with an impatient flap of his wings. "Wait! Just one more sec—what's that? *Zoltar?* What in all the bloomin' afterlife is a Zoltar?" Belfry paused and, I'd bet, held his breath while he waited for an answer—and then he let out a long, exasperated squeal of frustration before his tiny body went limp.

Which panicked me. Belfry was prone to drama-ish tendencies at the best of times, but the effort he was putting into being my conduit of sorts had been taking a toll. He was all I had, my last connection to anything supernatural. I couldn't bear losing him.

So I yanked him to my chest and tucked him into my soaking-wet sweater as I made a break for the hotel we were a week from being evicted right out of.

"Belfry!" I clung to his tiny body, rubbing my thumbs over the backs of his wings.

Belfry is a cotton ball bat. He's two inches from wing to wing of pure white bigmouth and minute yellow ears and snout, with origins stemming from Honduras, Nicaragua, and Costa Rica, where it's warm and humid.

Since we'd moved here to Seattle from the blazing-hot sun of Paris, Texas, he'd struggled with the cooler weather.

I was always finding ways to keep him warm, and now that he'd taxed himself by staying too long in the crappy weather we were having, plus using all his familiar energy to figure out who was trying to contact me, his wee self had gone into overload.

I reached for the credit card key to our hotel room in my skirt pocket and swiped it, my hands shaking. Slamming the door shut with the heel of my foot, I ran to the bathroom, flipped on the lights and set Belfry on a fresh white towel. His tiny body curled inward, leaving his wings tucked under him as pinhead-sized drops of water dripped on the towel.

Grabbing the blow dryer on the wall, I turned the setting to low and began swishing it over him from a safe distance so as not to knock him off the vanity top. "Belfry! Don't you poop on me now, buddy. I need you!" Using my index and my thumb, I rubbed along his rounded back, willing warmth into him.

"To the right," he ordered.

My fingers stiffened as my eyes narrowed, but I kept rubbing just in case.

He groaned. "Ahh, yeah. Riiight there."

"Belfry?"

"Yes, Wicked One?"

"Not the time to test my devotion."

"Are you fragile?"

"I wouldn't use the word fragile. But I would use mildly agitated and maybe even raw. If you're just joking around, knock it off. I've had all I can take in the way of shocks and upset this month."

He used his wings to push upward to stare at me with his melty chocolate eyes. "I wasn't testing your devotion. I was just depleted. Whoever this guy is, trying to get you on the line, he's determined. How did you manage to keep your fresh, dewy appearance with all that squawking in your ears all the time?"

I shrugged my shoulders and avoided my reflection in the mirror over the vanity. I didn't look so fresh and dewy anymore, and I knew it. I looked tired and devoid of interest in most everything around me. The bags under my eyes announced it to the world.

"We need to find a job, Belfry. We have exactly a week before my savings account is on E."

"So no lavish spending. Does that mean I'm stuck with the very average Granny Smith for dinner versus, say, a yummy pomegranate?"

I chuckled because I couldn't help it. I knew my laughter egged him on, but he was the reason I still got up every morning. Not that I'd ever tell him as much.

I reached for another towel and dried my hair, hoping it wouldn't frizz. "You get whatever is on the discount rack, buddy. Which should be incentive enough for you to help me find a job, lest you forgot how ripe those discounted bananas from the whole foods store really were."

"Bleh. Okay. Job. Onward ho. Got any leads?"

"The pharmacy in the center of town is looking for a cashier. It won't get us a cute house at the end of a cul-de-sac, but it'll pay for a decent enough studio. Do you want to come with or stay here and rest your weary wings?"

"Where you go, I go. I'm the tuna to your mayo."

"You have to stay in my purse, Belfry," I warned, scooping him up with two fingers to bring him to the closet with me to help me choose an outfit. "You can't wander out like you did at the farmers' market. I thought that jelly vendor was going to faint. This isn't Paris anymore. No one knows I'm a witch—" I sighed. "*Was* a witch, and no one especially knows you're a talking bat. Seattle is eclectic and all about the freedom to be you, but they haven't graduated to letting ex-witches leash their chatty bats outside of restaurants just yet."

"I got carried away. I heard 'mango chutney' and lost my teensy mind. I promise to stay in the dark hovel you call a purse—even if the British guy contacts me again."

"Forget the British guy and help me decide. Red Anne Klein skirt and matching jacket, or the less formal Blue Fly jeans and Gucci silk shirt in teal."

"You're not interviewing with Karl Lagerfeld. You're interviewing to sling sundries. Gum, potato chips, *People* magazine, maybe the occasional script for Viagra."

"It's an organic pharmacy right in that kitschy little knoll in town where all the food trucks and tattoo shops are. I'm not sure they make all-natural Viagra, but you sure sound disappointed we might have a roof over our heads."

"I'm disappointed you probably won't be wearing all those cute vintage clothes you're always buying at the thrift store if you work in a pharmacy."

"I haven't gotten the job yet, and if I do, I guess I'll just be the cutest cashier ever."

I decided on the Ann Klein. It never hurt to bring a touch of understated class, especially when the class had only cost me a total of twelve dollars.

As I laid out my wet clothes to dry on the tub and went about the business of putting on my best inter-view facade, I tried not to think about Belfry's broken communication with the British guy. There were times as a witch when I'd toiled over the souls who needed closure, sometimes to my detriment.

But I couldn't waste energy fretting over what I

couldn't fix. And if British Guy was hoping I could help him now, he was sorely misinformed.

Maybe the next time Belfry had an otherworldly connection, I'd ask him to put everyone in the afterlife on notice that Stevie Louise Cartwright was out of order.

Grabbing my purse from the hook on the back of the bathroom door, I smoothed my hands over my skirt and squared my shoulders.

"You ready, Belfry?"

"As I'll ever be."

"Ready, set, job!"

As I grabbed my raincoat and tucked Belfry into my purse, I sent up a silent prayer to the universe that my unemployed days were numbered.

NOTE FROM DAKOTA

I do hope you enjoyed this book, I'd so appreciate it if you'd help others enjoy it, too.

Recommend it. Please help other readers find this book by recommending it.

Review it. Please tell other readers why you liked this book by reviewing it at online retailers or your blog. Reader reviews help my books continue to be valued by distributors/resellers. I adore each and every reader who takes the time to write one!

If you love the book or leave a review, please email **dakota@dakotacassidy.com** so I can thank you with a personal email. Your support means more than you'll ever know! Thank you!"

ABOUT THE AUTHOR

Dakota Cassidy is a USA Today bestselling author with over thirty books. She writes laugh-out-loud cozy mysteries, romantic comedy, grab-some-ice erotic romance, hot and sexy alpha males, paranormal shifters, contemporary kick-ass women, and more.

Dakota was invited by Bravo TV to be the Bravo-holic for a week, wherein she snarked the hell out of all the Bravo shows. She received a starred review from Publishers Weekly for Talk Dirty to Me, won a Romantic Times Reviewers' Choice Award for Kiss and Hell, along with many review site recommended reads and reviewer top pick awards.

Dakota lives in the gorgeous state of Oregon with her real-life hero and her dogs, and she loves hearing from readers!

Visit Dakota's website at
http://www.dakotacassidy.com for more information.

A Lemon Layne Mystery, a Contemporary Cozy Mystery Series

1. Prawn of the Dead
2. Play That Funky Music White Koi

Witchless In Seattle Mysteries, a Paranormal Cozy Mystery series

1. Witch Slapped
2. Quit Your Witchin'
3. Dewitched
4. The Old Witcheroo
5. How the Witch Stole Christmas
6. Ain't Love a Witch
7. Good Witch Hunting
8. Witch Way Did He Go?

Nun of Your Business Mysteries, a Paranormal Cozy Mystery series

1. Then There Were Nun
2. Hit and Nun
3. House of the Rising Nun

Wolf Mates, a Paranormal Romantic Comedy series

1. An American Werewolf In Hoboken
2. What's New, Pussycat?
3. Gotta Have Faith
4. Moves Like Jagger
5. Bad Case of Loving You

A Paris, Texas Romance, a Paranormal Romantic Comedy series

1. Witched At Birth
2. What Not to Were
3. Witch Is the New Black
4. White Witchmas

Non-Series

Whose Bride Is She Anyway?
Polanski Brothers: Home of Eternal Rest
Sexy Lips 66

Accidentally Paranormal, a Paranormal Romantic Comedy series

Interview With an Accidental—a free introductory guide to the girls of the Accidentals!

1. The Accidental Werewolf
2. Accidentally Dead
3. The Accidental Human
4. Accidentally Demonic
5. Accidentally Catty

6. Accidentally Dead, Again

7. The Accidental Genie

8. The Accidental Werewolf 2: Something About Harry

9. The Accidental Dragon

10. Accidentally Aphrodite

11. Accidentally Ever After

12. Bearly Accidental

13. How Nina Got Her Fang Back

14. The Accidental Familiar

15. Then Came Wanda

16. The Accidental Mermaid

The Hell, a Paranormal Romantic Comedy series

1. Kiss and Hell

2. My Way to Hell

The Plum Orchard, a Contemporary Romantic Comedy series

1. Talk This Way

2. Talk Dirty to Me

3. Something to Talk About

4. Talking After Midnight

The Ex-Trophy Wives, a Contemporary Romantic Comedy series

1. You Dropped a Blonde On Me

2. Burning Down the Spouse

3. Waltz This Way

Fangs of Anarchy, a Paranormal Urban Fantasy series

1. Forbidden Alpha

2. Outlaw Alpha

25312453R00169